To
Jeanette
Love
mom & dad
Christmas
1974

THE BOBBSEY TWINS'
ADVENTURE IN THE COUNTRY

THE BOBBSEY TWINS
By Laura Lee Hope

"He's coming this way," Bert cried

The Bobbsey Twins' Adventure in the Country

By

LAURA LEE HOPE

GROSSET & DUNLAP

A NATIONAL GENERAL COMPANY

Publishers   *New York*

ISBN: 0–448–08002–8
© Grosset & Dunlap, Inc., 1961
All Rights Reserved

The Bobbsey Twins' Adventure in the Country

CONTENTS

CHAPTER I

FREDDIE'S SECRET

"HIGHER, Nan!" Flossie Bobbsey cried. "Make the water from the hose go higher!"

"Sure," Flossie's twin, Freddie, agreed. "We can jump much higher than that!"

The younger Bobbsey twins, Freddie and Flossie, were six. They had curly blond hair and wide blue eyes. Their older brother and sister, also twins, were Bert and Nan. They were twelve and had dark hair and eyes.

"Okay," Nan said. "Try this!" She raised the garden hose until the stream of water was about two feet from the ground. Freddie and Flossie took a long running start and cleared the water "jumping rope."

It was a warm day in June and Freddie, Flossie, and Nan had put on their bathing suits and were having fun in the back yard of their large rambling house in Lakeport.

"Ooh!" Flossie squealed. "Our clothes."

"I wish Bert would come," Nan said as she handed over the hose to her little sister so that she could take a turn. "He'll be hot after working in the lumberyard."

Mr. Bobbsey owned a lumber business on the shore of Lake Metoka. Sometimes, when he was not busy in school, Bert helped his father.

The children played with the water until it was Nan's turn again. Then she said, "Once more and we'll stop."

She adjusted the nozzle until a long straight stream poured out. "All right, Flossie, let's see you clear this!" she called.

"Wait! Here comes Bert!" Freddie exclaimed, as his brother entered the yard.

"Oh, Bert—!" Nan turned to greet her twin, forgetting that she held the hose. The stream of water shot through the air and struck with full force against a line of laundry strung across the rear of the yard!

"Ooh!" Flossie squealed. "Our clothes!"

At that moment the back door slammed and a plump colored woman came out onto the porch. "Who put that water on my clean clothes?" she asked in a stern voice.

"I did, Dinah," Nan confessed. "I'm sorry."

Dinah's expression softened. "Well," she admitted, "I know you didn't do it on purpose, Nan." The cook chuckled. "Those clothes'll be good and clean anyway." She went back into the kitchen.

Dinah Johnson and her husband Sam had lived in the Bobbsey home ever since Bert and Nan could remember. Dinah helped Mrs. Bobbsey at home with the cooking and cleaning, while Sam worked at the lumberyard. They were much-loved members of the household.

Bert grinned at Nan. "I'd like to get under that hose myself. I'll run in and put on my trunks."

"I'm going out front now and watch for the postman," Freddie announced.

"Why?" his twin wanted to know.

Freddie just looked mysterious and did not reply. Whistling, he sauntered around the corner of the house.

"I'll find out," Flossie offered. "I'll watch for Mr. Garret, too!"

When Flossie reached the front of the house she found Freddie seated on the porch steps, his chin in his hands. He was looking intently up the street.

Flossie sat down beside her twin. "Please, Freddie," she said coaxingly, "won't you tell me why you're waiting for the mail?"

"You'll know soon—I hope," Freddie replied. Then he jumped up and ran down to the sidewalk.

Up the street came friendly Mr. Garret. He carried a heavy leather pouch slung over one shoulder.

"Well now, Freddie," he said jovially when the little boy ran to meet him, "I'll see what I have for you." He began thumbing through a number of letters which he held in his hand.

Freddie stood on tiptoe watching. "There it is!" he cried excitedly. "I see it. It's that blue one!"

"But this is addressed to Mrs. Richard Bobbsey," Mr. Garret said solemnly. "I'll have to deliver it to her!"

"Please give it to me!" Freddie pleaded. "I'll take it to my mother right away!"

"All right," the postman agreed. "But don't lose it."

"I won't," Freddie assured him. "Thanks."

He ran as fast as he could up the walk and into the house. Flossie followed close behind. They dashed into the pleasant living room where Mrs. Bobbsey was sewing. She was a slender, pretty woman with a gay smile.

"Mommy," Flossie began breathlessly, "Freddie has a letter for you and he won't tell me what's in it!"

Her mother laughed and took the letter. "I don't see how he could know when it's sealed up."

"It's from Aunt Sarah, I'm sure it is," the little boy declared. "And I think I know what's inside. A big surprise!"

Mrs. Bobbsey slit open the envelope and took out the letter. "You're right," she said. "This is from Aunt Sarah, and she has some very interesting news. If you'll get Bert and Nan I'll read it to you all."

Aunt Sarah was the wife of Daniel Bobbsey, the twins' uncle. They lived on a farm near the little village of Meadowbrook. Their son Harry was the same age as Bert.

Freddie and Flossie ran from the room and in a few minutes were back with the older twins, all of them still in their bathing suits.

"Has something happened at Meadowbrook?" Nan asked.

"Are they coming to visit us?" Bert asked.

Mrs. Bobbsey held up her hands. "Not so fast children! Something is going to happen, but not here. We've been invited to visit *them* at Meadowbrook!"

"Super!" cried Bert.

"Goody, goody!" Flossie cried, clapping her hands. "When are we going?"

"Aunt Sarah suggests that we come before next Saturday because of something special she wants us to do."

"What is it?" Nan asked.

"Aunt Sarah says there's going to be an auction in Meadowbrook. A certain article is being offered for sale which she thinks we'd like to buy."

"What's an auction?" Flossie wanted to know.

"Well," her mother began, "an auction is a public sale of different articles. And people who want to buy the things tell the auctioneer how much they want to pay."

Flossie still looked puzzled.

"Then," Bert chimed in, "the man running the sale sells the article to the person who will pay the highest price."

"You mean they fight?" Flossie asked excitedly.

"Oh goodness, no," Mrs. Bobbsey said, laughing along with the older twins. "It's not so bad as that!"

"I know," Bert said, jumping up. "We'll have our own auction right now."

"Hooray!" cried Freddie. "You be the auctioneer, Bert!"

"And I'll get one of my dolls for you to sell!" Flossie cried as she ran off.

By the time she returned with the doll, Bert had placed a newspaper on the piano bench and was standing on top of it. The younger twins, Nan, and Mrs. Bobbsey settled themselves to watch.

"All right, folks," Bert said importantly. "What am I bid for this beautiful, perfect, genuine rag doll? Do I hear five dollars?"

"Five dollars!" Flossie shouted. "That's too much!"

"And the doll's not perfect, either," Freddie popped up. "She's lost her right arm!"

The children giggled as Bert examined the genuine rag doll. "Well, so she has," he admitted. "Do I hear two dollars for this almost-perfect doll? . . . Do I hear *one* dollar? Only one dollar for this lovely doll?"

"Twenty-five cents!" came a cry from Freddie.

"Twenty-five cents?" Bert, the auctioneer, shouted. "Only twenty-five cents for this valuable doll?"

There was silence.

"Last call," Bert cried. "Okay, twenty-five cents," he said, shaking his head. "Going for twenty-five cents. . . . Going . . . Going . . . GONE, for twenty-five cents!"

"Where's it gone?" Flossie begged eagerly.

"Nowhere," Nan broke in. "Gone means it's sold."

"Yes," came Bert's voice. "Sold for twenty-five cents to the gentleman in the front row!"

"It's mine!" Freddie cried as he accepted the doll.

"But it's *my* doll!" Flossie wailed.

"Don't worry, dear," Nan comforted her. "This is only a pretend auction."

"Yes," said Freddie, walking over to his twin. "And I'm only using pretend money. I was buying the doll so I could give it to you!"

"Oh, thank you," Flossie cried. "I like auctions!" She hugged her rag doll.

Mrs. Bobbsey smiled. "I think you'll enjoy the auction at Meadowbrook much more now," she said warmly.

"It does sound like fun," Nan remarked. "But how does Aunt Sarah know what we'd like to buy?"

"I guess that's a mystery you children will have to work on," Mrs. Bobbsey said teasingly. She knew the twins loved new mysteries to solve.

"Another mystery is how Freddie knew Aunt Sarah was going to write this letter," Bert said, giving his little brother an inquiring glance.

Freddie hung his head. "I heard Daddy tell Mother the other day that Aunt Sarah and Uncle Daniel were going to ask us to come to Meadowbrook. I thought I'd surprise you!"

Mrs. Bobbsey stood up. "This is Monday. If we're going to leave for Meadowbrook by Friday, we'll have to start planning."

When the twins' father came home to lunch they told him about the invitation. "We are going, aren't we, Daddy?" Flossie asked eagerly.

"Yes, my little fat fairy," he replied. "I think a visit on the farm will do you all good."

Mr. Bobbsey called his small daughter by this nickname to tease her. He called Freddie his little fat fireman because the little boy loved to play with toy fire engines, and often declared he was going to be a fireman when he grew up.

"But aren't you going with us, Daddy?" Freddie inquired.

Mr. Bobbsey shook his head. "I can't get away this week. But I'll be there as soon as I can."

Aunt Sarah had invited Dinah to come with the family, so it was decided that Mrs. Bobbsey and Dinah would take the children to Meadowbrook on the Friday morning train.

"Unfortunately there's no diner on the train," said Mr. Bobbsey.

"Will you pack us a lunch, Dinah?" Flossie asked as the jolly cook passed a bowl of fruit.

"Why sure, honey," Dinah agreed.

The next few days were very busy. Nan went with her mother to the shop for shorts, dungarees, and sweaters for all the children. Suitcases were brought down from the attic.

The day before they were to leave Freddie and Flossie looked over their toys to decide which ones they would take with them.

"I'll have to take my pumper," Freddie said.

"You never can tell when a farm will catch fire and I'll have to put it out. And I think I'll take my new baseball cap, too." He ran into his room and returned with a navy-blue cap which he tossed onto the heap.

"I'm only going to take two dolls," Flossie stated. "Linda and Bessie."

Bessie was only five inches tall. She was dressed as a ballerina in a fluffy white dress and on her feet were tiny black ballet slippers.

"We have to take Snoop, too," Freddie reminded his mother. Snoop was the black cat which had been given to Freddie when the little boy had been locked in a department store by mistake. This adventure happened in THE BOBBSEY TWINS OF LAKEPORT.

Mrs. Bobbsey looked doubtful. "I'm not sure we can take Snoop."

Freddie's face fell. "But we have to!" he said desperately. "Snoop rescued me. We can't leave him here all by himself!"

"All right," his mother agreed. "We'll have to get a carrying basket for him."

Bert hurried to the store and returned with a wicker basket. It had plenty of air holes so that Snoop would be able to breathe, and a top which was easy to take off.

Early Friday morning Sam brought the station wagon around to the front of the house. He and Mr. Bobbsey and Bert carried the suitcases out and stacked them in the rear. Then the family and Dinah piled in and Sam drove toward the station. Freddie held Snoop's basket in his lap.

As they neared the depot, Dinah suddenly gave a little cry.

"What's the matter?" asked Mr. Bobbsey.

"I left our box of lunch on the kitchen table!" Dinah moaned. "All those good sandwiches!"

"And no food on the train!" Bert spoke up.

Mr. Bobbsey looked at his watch. "We're almost at the station now," he said. "Sam can let us out and then go back for the lunch."

Sam drove up to the station platform and they all hurriedly got out. When the last suitcase was on the ground, the colored man swung the car around and sped back to the Bobbsey house. The minutes went by.

"Mother," Freddie said nervously, "it's almost time for the train. Do you think Sam can get back in time?"

CHAPTER II

THE BOBBSEY twins began to pace the railroad platform nervously. They would be starved before reaching Meadowbrook!

To get everyone's mind off the subject, Bert said, "I see a weighing machine. Let's get weighed. The sign says you get a fortune too for a penny."

The twins went inside and Nan stepped onto the machine while Bert dropped a penny in the slot. There was a whirring noise and a small card dropped down into a slot.

With a giggle Nan handed it to Bert. The card read:

You weigh 92.

Beware a dark man who is close to you.

"It must be you, Bert," Nan said, pretending to be frightened, and her brother laughed.

When Bert got his card, he found he weighed

13

five pounds more than his twin. His fortune read:

A blond woman in your family will cause trouble.

"I guess that's Flossie." Bert chuckled. "I'll keep my eye on her!"

At this moment they heard the train whistle far down the track.

"Mommy!" Flossie cried. "Here comes the train, and Sam isn't back!"

"Never mind," Mrs. Bobbsey replied. "We'll just have to forget about lunch."

"But I want to eat!" Freddie said. "I'm hungry now."

By this time the engine had roared into the station and people were getting off the coaches. A conductor standing at the nearby steps helped the passengers getting off.

When the last person had walked down, he turned to the group on the platform. "All aboard!"

"I guess you'll have to get on, Mary," Mr. Bobbsey advised his wife, after he had kissed his family. "I'll see you in a few days."

"Here comes Sam!" Freddie shouted. He pointed to the colored man sprinting toward them across the parking lot.

"All aboard!" the conductor warned.

Mrs. Bobbsey and the twins climbed up the

steps. Dinah hesitated. At last Sam dashed up and put the big white box in her hand and she stepped aboard.

"Thanks, Sam! Good-by," the twins chorused, as the train started to move. Sam waved, his white teeth showing in a big grin.

The conductor, seeing Dinah's box of lunch, smiled and said, "Maybe you folks would like to go into the club part of this car. See the table and four chairs, and seats across the aisle."

"Fine. We'll sit there."

The conductor suggested that they leave their luggage in the coach, so only Snoop and the lunch were carried into the club section. Freddie set Snoop's basket on the table. Men and women passengers smiled.

"You children can use the table," Mrs. Bobbsey said. "Dinah and I will sit across the aisle."

The twins settled themselves as the train began to gather speed.

"I wonder if Snoop is scared of the train," Freddie mused. He took off the basket top and put in his hand to pet the cat.

At the same instant Snoop gave a great leap and jumped to the floor. Then he dashed up the aisle toward the other end of the car.

"Catch him!" Freddie screamed.

The other passengers looked startled as Bert raced after the fleeing cat. When Snoop found a closed door in front of him he gave another leap and landed on the back of the last seat. From there he jumped to the luggage rack overhead.

"Here, Snoop. Nice kitty," Bert coaxed softly. "Come on down."

But Snoop crouched on a man's briefcase and stared down. Bert climbed to the arm of the seat and reached toward the cat. Snoop moved just out of range. Bert got down.

"Oh!" Flossie cried. "Will the conductor put poor Snoop off the train?"

At that moment the door opened and the conductor came in. When he saw the smiling faces of the passengers, he looked puzzled. Bert looked out the window, hoping the trainman would not notice the cat on the rack.

But Snoop was not satisfied to leave things as they were. He gave a flying leap and landed on the conductor's shoulder!

"What's this?" the man cried.

Freddie ran down the aisle and stopped in front of the conductor. Snoop by this time was perched on the man's shoulder, waving his tail across the trainman's face.

"It's Snoop, Mr. Conductor," Freddie explained. "He's a very nice cat, honestly. You won't put him off the train, will you?"

"Not if you have a basket for him," the man

replied with a broad smile. He took Snoop in his arms and followed Freddie back down the aisle.

"You can call me Mac," he said when Freddie introduced him to Mrs. Bobbsey, Dinah, and the girls.

"Maybe Snoop is hungry," Mac went on, rubbing the cat under the chin and making him purr. "I might get him something from the kitchen."

"A kitchen!" Nan exclaimed. "I thought this train had no diner?"

"You must have been looking at an old time-table," the conductor stated. "We have a very up-to-date kitchen. Come along and I'll show you."

With Bert carrying Snoop, he led the four twins through several cars to the door of the narrow kitchen. The children were interested to see the gleaming cupboards and counters and the cooks in starched white aprons and caps busily preparing food.

"What's that you're holding?" one of them asked with a wink at Bert. "Something for the soup?"

"Oh no!" Freddie cried in alarm.

Mac chuckled. "We thought you might have a bit of fish for this extra passenger," he said.

In another minute Snoop was daintily eating from a saucer which the cook had placed on the floor in the aisle. The sight reminded the twins of their own box of sandwiches.

They thanked Mac and the cook. Then, with Snoop held once more by Bert, they made their way back to the club section of their car.

"Snoop has made us all hungry, Mother," Nan said when they reached their places again and put the cat back in his basket. "Is it time for lunch?"

"Yes. I think we may as well eat now."

After Dinah had spread the tempting sandwiches out on the table a man came down the aisle carrying a large metal basket. "Milk, coffee, tea, tomato juice," he called.

"We'd like milk, please." Mrs. Bobbsey signaled him.

The man opened little cartons of milk, stuck a straw into each one, and passed them to the children. "I like milk from a box," Flossie announced.

When the sandwiches were gone, Nan passed the cookies and fruit.

"I can hardly wait to get to Meadowbrook," Flossie said. "Aren't we almost there?"

Mrs. Bobbsey looked at her watch. "We should be there in about an hour. What do you children want to do while you're at the farm?"

"Go to the auction," said Freddie. "I want to see that auctioneer man who talks so fast."

"I'm going to plant a garden," Flossie said. "All the things I like—peas, beans, ice cream—"

"You can't plant ice cream!" Freddie interrupted and they all laughed.

"I mean things you put in ice cream, like strawberries," Flossie defended herself.

"One thing you must be careful of," Mrs. Bobbsey spoke up. "That's Uncle Daniel's bull. Never let him out of his pen."

The twins promised to obey. Presently Flossie's eyes grew heavy. She rested her head on the table and soon was fast asleep. Before long Freddie was nodding drowsily also. Mrs. Bobbsey and Dinah had been reading books.

Nan looked at Bert. "Let's play a game," she suggested.

"Okay. What'll it be?"

"Let's watch out the window and spot things beginning with the letters of the alphabet," Nan proposed.

"All right. You begin."

Nan peered from the window for a few minutes. Then she looked up at the sky. "An airplane!" she cried. "Now you have to find something starting with B."

"I know a way to make the game harder," Bert suggested. "You have to see something which would be found on a farm!"

Nan agreed to this. "I'll start again." She scanned the countryside as the train sped along. "We're going so fast, it's hard to see anything small," she complained.

Just then the train slowed as it went through the main street of a little village. "An axe!" Nan called, pointing to the tool which was leaning against the side of an old barn.

"Good!" said Bert. "Now it's my turn to find a B."

The twins gazed out the window for a while,

then Bert cried, "I see a bridge and a barn. They both might be found on a farm!"

The game went on. Nan saw a cow, then Bert spotted a dog running across a field. Next Nan pointed to a woman walking toward a farmhouse with a basket of eggs on her arm.

"Now it's your turn with an F," Nan announced.

At that moment a small flock of birds rose from a field. As they flew low over the high grass Bert exclaimed:

"Pheasants!"

Nan looked startled then burst into giggles. "Silly!" she said. "Pheasant doesn't begin with an F!"

Bert grinned sheepishly. "I guess you're right, Nan." He turned to the window again, then announced, "There's a flag. Every farm should have a flag!"

Nan started to protest but just then their friend Mac the conductor came into the car. "Next stop Meadowbrook!" he called. "Passengers for Meadowbrook out this way!"

Mrs. Bobbsey closed her book and called across the aisle, "Freddie! Flossie! Wake up! We're coming into Meadowbrook."

The small twins sat up, sleepily rubbing their eyes. Dinah picked up the box which had held the lunch and walked with Bert to get the luggage.

The young twins had their noses pressed to the car window as the train drew into the station. "I see them!" Freddie shouted. "There's Uncle Daniel! And Harry!"

He slipped off the seat and hurried to the door, with the others following close behind.

Uncle Daniel, tall and strong-looking, was at the steps with Harry to help them down to the platform with their luggage. "My, it's good to see you!" they said.

As the train began to move off Freddie suddenly let out a scream. "Snoop! We forgot Snoop!" he yelled.

CHAPTER III

FRISKY, THE RUNAWAY

FLOSSIE took up the cry. "Snoop! Please get Snoop!"

As soon as Bert realized their pet was still in the club car, he ran alongside the train, hoping to jump up on the steps.

"Bert, come back!" Mrs. Bobbsey cried. "You'll get hurt!"

Her son stopped uncertainly. The last car of the train was passing him when he looked up and saw Mac the conductor standing on the steps. The man was holding Snoop's basket!

"Catch!" he called. Mac leaned down and tossed the wicker cage into Bert's outstretched hands. "Here's your friend," he said. "Have a good time at Meadowbrook!" Then with a wave the kindly conductor climbed the steps again and the train gradually disappeared in the distance.

23

Freddie ran up and lifted Snoop from the basket. "Poor Snoop!" he said. "You'll be at the farm soon and then you can run around and play with Harry's cat!"

"Yes." Harry's ruddy, tanned face broke into a grin. "Fluffy gets lonesome being the only cat on the farm!"

Uncle Daniel laughed. "Come, get in the car, everyone," he said. "Aunt Sarah is waiting for us at home."

"How is everything on the farm?" Bert asked Harry.

"Great, and I have some special news for you."

"What is it?"

"Major won first prize in the County Stock Show!" Harry announced proudly.

"Who is Major?" Freddie wanted to know. "Can we play with him?"

Harry chuckled. "I don't think you'd want to play with Major. He's our bull!"

"Oh!" said Flossie. She had already decided to admire Major from a safe distance!

The farm was not far from the village, and in a short while Uncle Daniel turned into the lane. It was bordered on each side by hedges of boxwood. The neat gravel driveway led up to a comfortable-looking white farmhouse. When the car stopped, a side door of the house opened.

Aunt Sarah Bobbsey and Martha, the family cook, came out to meet the Lakeport Bobbseys.

Aunt Sarah was short and rather plump. Martha was tall and thin with a twinkle in her blue eyes. After greetings were over, Aunt Sarah said:

"Just go up to your old rooms. I know you must want to get into country clothes!"

"Hurry down!" Harry urged. "I'll take you to see Major."

It was a matter of only a few minutes until the twins came downstairs again, dressed in shirts and jeans, for fun on the farm. Harry led them outdoors.

"What gorgeous flowers!" Nan exclaimed, walking over to admire the beds of roses.

"May I pick one?" Flossie asked.

"Sure. Go ahead," Harry replied. "The more you pick them, the bigger the next flowers will be!"

Flossie pulled off a huge pink bloom and stuck it into the buttonhole of her blouse. "Isn't it bee-yoo-ti-ful?" she asked, twirling around for them all to see.

They nodded, then Harry remarked, "Major's down beside the barn. Let's go!"

The five children ran across the green lawn and over to the big barnyard. In a separate pen next to the white barn was the prize bull. He snorted and swung his head up and down when Harry introduced him.

"He acts as if he wants to play with us!" Freddie said in delight.

"You'd better stay away from him," Bert advised. "Bulls can be dangerous."

Reluctantly Freddie left Major and followed Harry and the other children over to the chicken yard. Hundreds of white hens were running about, busily pecking at the ground.

"Want to see some excitement?" Harry asked his cousins.

"Sure," Bert said for the group.

Harry picked up a bucket of grain standing nearby. Then he scattered the contents in a wide arc. Instantly they were surrounded by chickens. *Cluck, cluck, cluck.* The birds cackled loudly as they pushed and shoved to get at the grain.

At one side of the chicken yard, Flossie noticed a small pen. "Why are those chickens all by themselves?" she wanted to know.

"Those aren't chickens," Harry replied. "They're my new homing pigeons. Some day I'm going to take them way out in the country and send them back with a note to Mother or Martha!"

"What do you mean?" Flossie asked, curious.

Harry explained that homing pigeons can be taken long distances from where they live and when released find their way home again. "They're sometimes used to carry messages during a war. A little capsule with a note in it is fastened to the pigeon's leg."

"Let's try it now," Freddie suggested eagerly.

Harry shook his head. "You have to let them loose away from their home. We'll do it some day when we go on a picnic."

The children turned back to the barnyard. "This is Frisky," Harry said, walking up to a little black-and-white calf which was tied to a stake near the barn. As the boy stroked her, the little animal rubbed her head affectionately against his shoulder.

"She's nice," Freddie said admiringly. "May I ride her?"

"You don't ride calves," Harry explained, "only ponies and horses."

"Then may I take her for a walk?"

"Calves don't walk either," Flossie volunteered. "They run." She remembered pictures in her story books about calves kicking up their heels.

The other children followed Harry into the barn to see the horses but Freddie lingered beside the calf.

"I don't see why I shouldn't just take her for a little walk around the yard," he said to himself. "That wouldn't hurt anything."

Quickly the little boy slipped the rope off the stake and put the loop around his wrist. "Come on, Frisky," he said, "let's take a walk."

The calf went along quietly by Freddie's side for a few minutes. "I wish Flossie would come out and see me," he thought with a giggle.

But suddenly Frisky caught sight of the open gate and the green lawn beyond. She kicked up her back heels and made for the gate. Freddie was dragged along behind her.

"Stop, Frisky!" he called. "I can't run so fast!"

But the little calf paid no attention and continued her dash toward the front of the house. Freddie's cries reached the ears of his mother and Aunt Sarah who were talking on the porch.

Aunt Sarah ran down the steps. "Let go, Freddie! Let go!" she cried.

But the loop was fast around Freddie's wrist and he could not get it off. At that moment Frisky dashed around a small tree, winding the rope as she went. Freddie fell to the ground at the foot of the tree.

Then just as Mrs. Bobbsey and Aunt Sarah reached Freddie, the rope slipped over the calf's head and she skittered happily away.

"Freddie dear," his mother cried, "are you hurt?"

Freddie sat up and rubbed his arm. "I—I

guess not," he said. "Can you catch Frisky?"

"Never mind the calf," Aunt Sarah said quickly. "Let's see your wrist."

When she saw that the little boy's arm was red and scratched, they hurried him into the house for antiseptic and bandage.

In the meantime, Harry was showing the other twins two stout farm horses. "We don't use them much any more, but Dad doesn't like to part with them. They're pretty old. Their names are Billy and Betty."

"I think they're bee-yoo-ti-ful," Flossie said staunchly.

Just then the sound of Freddie's cries reached the barn and the children ran to the door.

"What is Freddie doing with that calf?" Bert asked in bewilderment.

"Frisky's running away with him!" Harry exclaimed and started in pursuit.

But by the time Harry had reached the front lawn, Frisky had broken loose and Freddie was being led into the house. "See if you can catch that calf, Bert," Mrs. Bobbsey called over her shoulder.

Flossie ran into the house to see how Freddie was, but the older twins and Harry turned to see where Frisky had gone. The black-and-white calf was standing in the vegetable garden, eating some tender young shoots.

"Hey, get out of there!" Harry cried, running toward the garden.

At the sound of Harry's voice Frisky took to her heels again, with Harry, Bert, and Nan after her. She ran across the vegetable garden and into the orchard.

"Maybe we can trap her," Harry proposed. "You and Nan go around one side, Bert. I'll go around the other."

Carefully the twins crept among the trees. Frisky stood still and eyed them warily. Then, just as the children reached her and Harry put out a hand to grab the rope, the calf bounded away!

But this time she ran toward the barn. "Good!" Bert said. "I guess she's ready to go home."

The three followed the runaway calf and when she headed into the barnyard, Harry heaved a sigh of relief. "She'll be all right now," he commented.

When the children had almost reached the barn, Freddie ran out of the house followed by Flossie. The little boy's wrist was bandaged.

"I'm awf'ly sorry, Harry," Freddie said as he came up to the others. "I didn't mean to let Frisky run away. I held on as long as I could!"

"That's all right, Freddie," Harry said. "Frisky's back safe and sound."

But he had spoken too soon. Frisky still had not had enough freedom. When Harry reached for the rope to tie it to the stake the calf gave a leap and was off again!

"Catch her!" Freddie yelled.

This time Frisky dashed across the pasture and into a thicket which bordered it. When the children reached the spot where she had disappeared, they could hear the little animal thrashing through the brush.

Then came the sound of a *splash!* The twins

turned questioning eyes to Harry. "What was that?" Bert asked.

"I'm afraid Frisky has jumped into the river!" Harry replied.

"Oh, can she swim?" Nan asked worriedly.

"I suppose so, but she'll have a hard time in the swift current," Harry replied.

CHAPTER IV

A SURPRISE FLAVOR

"OH NO!" Freddie wailed at Harry's suggestion that Frisky had jumped into the river. "She —she can't drown!"

"Maybe she didn't go far," Bert said. "Let's see if we can find her."

The little group dashed through the tangle of bushes and tall grass until they reached the river bank. There was no calf in sight either on the shore or in the water.

Freddie's eyes filled with tears. "It's all my fault if Frisky is drowned!" he cried. "I didn't mean to hurt her! I just wanted to take her for a walk!"

"Maybe that splash was from something else," Harry said encouragingly. "I see a tree limb floating downstream. Let's hunt for Frisky all along the shore."

But although the five children pushed their

way through the dense growth along the bank they did not find Frisky and finally turned back.

"Maybe the calf circled around and is home in the barnyard now," Nan said hopefully. Freddie's expression brightened somewhat.

But when they reached the barn again there was no sign of the little calf. Sadly the children returned to the house and reported their failure to find Frisky.

"Never mind, Freddie," Uncle Daniel said kindly. "I know where I can get another calf."

"But it won't be Frisky!" Freddie objected.

Aunt Sarah attempted to get Freddie's mind off the lost calf by mentioning the auction to which they were going the next day. "You'll like it," she said.

"Will the man who talks real fast be there?" Flossie asked.

Aunt Sarah smiled. "Yes indeed."

"What is the special thing you want us to see, Aunt Sarah?" Nan asked.

"You'll have to wait and find out," her aunt replied mysteriously.

"Do you know what it is, Mommy?" Flossie asked.

Mrs. Bobbsey laughed. "I have a good idea," she said teasingly. "But I'm not going to tell, so there's no use coaxing!"

But still Freddie did not smile. Bert looked

anxiously at Harry who responded by standing up. "Come on, Freddie," he urged. "Let's you and Bert and I walk down to the Holden farm. It's not far and my friend Tom has a younger brother just about your age. His name is Roy."

Freddie looked a little happier. "Okay," he agreed. "We can look for Frisky on the way."

After the boys had left and the grownups had gone out for a stroll around the farm, Nan sighed. "I wish we could think of something to cheer up Freddie," she said to her sister.

Flossie thought a minute then suggested that they ask Dinah. "Maybe she will know what to do."

The two girls ran to the kitchen where Dinah and Martha were seated at the table shelling peas. Nan and Flossie explained how sad Freddie was about the loss of Frisky.

"We might cheer him up with some home-made ice cream," Dinah suggested.

"You mean we'll make it?" Nan asked.

"Yes. I'll show you how. All right, Martha?"

Martha nodded. "There's just about time before supper. Better make it out on the back porch. We'll be busy in here."

Dinah set out the cream, eggs, and sugar on a table on the shady porch. "You can mix it in this," she directed, bringing out a large yellow bowl. "I'll fix the freezer for you."

Carefully Nan mixed the cream and eggs. Then Flossie had an idea. "Let's make this extra-special ice cream," she proposed. "Let's put in some strawberries!"

"I thought we were going to make chocolate," Nan said. "Dinah is getting it ready now."

"I know," Flossie said with a giggle, "but if we put in strawberries too, it'll be even more special!"

Nan agreed, though a little doubtfully, and the two girls ran out to the strawberry patch.

When Dinah came out onto the porch with the chocolate syrup she was surprised to find Nan and Flossie gone. "I'll just see how it tastes," she told herself, and picked up a spoon. She dipped it into the creamy mixture.

"They've forgotten the sugar." She chuckled. "I'll fix it and they won't know the difference." She added the correct amount of sugar and went back into the kitchen.

In a few minutes Nan and Flossie returned from their errand. "Let's wash the berries in this water," Flossie proposed, pointing to an outside tap. "Then the ice cream will be a s'prise to Dinah too!"

This was quickly done, and the girls walked up onto the porch. As they did so, Flossie spied her ballerina doll on the floor.

"Oh dear!" she cried. "Bessie must have fallen out when Bert and Harry took in the suitcases!" She picked up the doll and examined her. "She's sort of mussed up," Flossie observed, "but I think she'll be all right."

In the meantime, Nan had added the sugar she had not put in before, the chocolate syrup, and the strawberries to the ice-cream mixture. Now she went into the kitchen to report to Dinah that they were ready for the freezer.

Flossie, with Bessie clutched in her arms, peered in the bowl. "Freddie likes it nice and sweet," she thought. "I'll just put in some more sugar." With that she picked up the sugar dish and dumped a generous amount into the ice cream.

Dinah came out with the freezer. "I've put the ice and salt around the can," she explained. "Just pour the ice cream into the can, put on the lid, and keep turning the crank. I have to get back now to the kitchen. I've got a cake in the oven."

Nan and Flossie took turns grinding the freezer crank and after a while it became hard to do. Dinah came to look. She said the mixture had thickened and pronounced the ice cream finished.

"Come and get ready for supper," Aunt Sarah called. "The boys are back and they're hungry!"

"Did they find Frisky?" Nan asked.

"Unfortunately, no."

Tears came to Flossie's eyes. "I hope Frisky finds a nice barn to stay in tonight."

Later when all the Bobbseys were at the table the twins' mother asked, "What did you girls do when the boys went to the Holden farm?"

Flossie looked at Nan and winked. "You'll find out pretty soon," she said. "Nan and I made a s'prise for everybody!"

"A coat for our rooster?" Harry teased.

"You can't eat that," said Flossie, giggling.

"I know," Bert spoke up. "An apple-tree pie."

Freddie, although he still felt sad when he thought about the missing Frisky, said, "Flossie and Nan made something with strawberries."

The girls looked at each other. How close Freddie had come to guessing their secret!

When the delicious dinner of country ham and candied sweet potatoes had been eaten, Martha brought in a large glass bowl and put it in front of Aunt Sarah.

"This is the s'prise!" Flossie explained.

"Ice cream!" Freddie cried. "Oh, boy! You made it?"

Aunt Sarah served the dessert. She took a spoonful and an odd look came over her face. "It's —er—quite good," she murmured.

Next Nan tasted her dessert. She put down her spoon. "Goodness!" she said, "this is too sweet!" She looked at her sister. "Did you put sugar in the ice cream, Flossie?"

"Why yes. I thought it needed some more."

Suddenly Dinah, who was bringing in the cake, burst out, "Lawsy me! Sugar! I put some in, too!"

Bert grinned. "New flavor, folks. Chocolate-strawberry-sugar ice cream."

At that moment Uncle Daniel looked at something on his spoon. "And what's this?" he exclaimed.

Flossie leaned over to see, then burst into giggles. "It's Bessie's dancing slipper!" she gasped. "It must have slipped off when I was putting in the sugar!"

"Ho, ho!" Bert cried. "That's better yet. Chocolate-strawberry-sugar-dancing-slipper ice cream!"

This was too much for the whole Bobbsey family and Dinah. They burst into laughter. Martha came in to see what the fun was about. She too chuckled when she saw what Uncle Daniel had found in the dessert.

Dinner ended with everyone in high spirits. But presently Freddie became solemn again. "Can't we do something more about finding Frisky?" he asked Uncle Daniel, who was in the living room.

"Don't worry, Freddie. I believe the little calf can take care of herself. She'll probably find a new home."

This gave Freddie an idea. Flossie had mentioned that Frisky might go to another barn. "Uncle Daniel," he said, "could we phone to all the neighbors and ask them if the calf is visiting their cows?"

Uncle Daniel put an arm around his little nephew. "That's a good idea, Freddie," and he called upstairs, "Harry, come down here and do some phoning for your cousin."

When Harry arrived, Freddie explained the plan. At once Harry put in calls to all the farmhouses within a radius of three miles. None of the owners had seen Frisky but they promised to look for him.

Freddie waited anxiously for word, but bedtime came and still no one had called. Sadly, Freddie went upstairs and undressed.

"Maybe there'll be good news in the morning," his mother told him, as she kissed her small son goodnight.

Snoop was put into a padded box in the kitchen, and presently everyone went to bed.

It seemed to Freddie that he had been asleep for a long time when he was awakened by pounding on the front door. He heard Uncle Daniel go downstairs to answer it, then exclaim, "You found her!" It sounded as if someone was talking about Frisky!

Freddie jumped out of bed excitedly and ran to the top of the stairs. A strange man was speaking to Uncle Daniel.

"You didn't phone me, but my wife happened to be talking to Mrs. Holden, and she told her about your lost calf."

Freddie raced down the stairs.

"I went into the barn," the stranger continued,

"and there was this strange calf. Is it yours?"

By now Freddie could see a truck with a calf standing in it. He dashed outside and pulled himself up onto the truck.

"Frisky!" he yelled. "You're back!"

"That's Frisky all right," Uncle Daniel replied. "Thanks for returning her. Freddie, this is Mr. Peter Burns, one of our neighbors."

Freddie leaned down and shook hands with Mr. Burns. "Oh thanks a million," he said. Then he hugged Frisky.

"Freddie, how would you like to get your bathrobe and slippers and then help us put the calf in the barn?" Uncle Daniel asked.

"Oh boy, would I!" Freddie answered.

By this time the other children had awakened and Freddie told them the news. There was great rejoicing that Frisky was back on the farm and all of them went to help put Frisky to bed.

Everyone slept peacefully, but around midnight Flossie began to have a silly dream. She thought Frisky came prancing into the house and began to play the piano! Flossie awoke, smiling to herself. The idea of a musical black-and-white calf!

Then suddenly Flossie sat up in bed and listened. The house was dark but someone *was* playing the piano!

CHAPTER V

GOING, GOING, GONE!

"NAN! NAN!" Flossie jumped out of bed and tugged at her sister's covers.

Sleepily Nan sat up. "Wh-what's the matter?" she murmured.

"It's all dark," Flossie whispered, "but somebody's downstairs playing the piano!"

Nan stumbled from her bed and followed Flossie into the hall. They listened. The first floor was dark and everything was quiet.

"You must have been dreaming," Nan said, "but I'll get Uncle Daniel and we'll look."

He turned on the lower hall light and hurried with the girls to the living room. No one was there. But Nan noticed that a sheet of music which had been on the piano rack now lay on the floor.

"Somebody knocked that down," she said. "Flossie, was this the tune the person was playing?"

43

"I-I don't think so," Flossie answered. "It was only like lots of scales all at once."

Uncle Daniel smiled, and Flossie knew he thought she had been dreaming. She did not mention Frisky as he turned out the lights and they all went back upstairs.

When the girls were in their room once more, Flossie said, "Nan, I *did* hear the piano—really I did."

Nan smiled. "Then that's another mystery for us to solve. Just think, Flossie, we haven't been here one whole day yet, and we've had three mysteries."

"One got solved tonight—Frisky," said Flossie. "And tomorrow we'll go to the auction. But we might never know about the piano."

"Unless it gets played again," Nan answered sleepily.

The next morning at breakfast Harry said he had a suggestion for Sunday. "Let's have a picnic after church—just us children."

"That would be fun," Nan said. "We'll fix the food today."

Bert asked where they would have the picnic.

"We might go out to the grove near the quarry," Harry replied. "May we, Mother?"

"All right," she consented.

"Dad, will you take us?"

Uncle Daniel nodded. "How about going in

the hay wagon? Billy and Betty need exercise."

"A hay wagon!" Bert exclaimed. "That sounds great!"

"I'll call my friends Tom Holden and Bud Stout right away," Harry said. "Tom can bring his little brother to play with Freddie."

"Aren't there any girls in this neighborhood?" Nan asked.

Harry looked sheepish. "I guess there are," he said, "but I don't usually play with girls."

Aunt Sarah leaned over and patted Nan's hand. "There are some very nice girls near here," she remarked. "I'll call Patty Manners and Kim Harold. I think you'll like them and I know they enjoy picnics."

The morning passed quickly with arrangements for the picnic next day. The boys and girls on the nearby farms eagerly accepted the invitations. Dinah and Martha planned what they would prepare for the lunch. Bert, Freddie, and Harry were busy in the barn, currying Billy and Betty.

"There, they look keen!" Harry observed as he put down the curry-comb and stood back to admire the sleek farm horses.

Everyone bathed and dressed for the auction. After lunch Uncle Daniel, Aunt Sarah, Mrs. Bobbsey, and the five children climbed into the station wagon for the trip. The vehicle was crowded, so the older children took turns holding Freddie and Flossie on their laps.

"Oh!" Bert pretended to groan when Flossie plumped herself down on his knees. "Now I know why Dad calls you his little fat fairy!"

"I'm heavy, too," Freddie bragged, bouncing up and down on Harry's lap.

Suddenly Harry spread his knees apart and Freddie tumbled to the floor. "You weigh so much I can't even hold you," Harry said teasingly.

The auction was to be held in Meadowbrook. Uncle Daniel parked on the town square and led the way into a tent which had been erected on the green. At the far end was a raised platform. On it was a small table. A man stood behind it with a wooden gavel in his hand.

Near the platform were articles of all descriptions. There were tables and chairs, lamps with broken shades, baby buggies, books, records, and stacks of dishes and glassware.

"Those are the things for sale," Aunt Sarah explained. "The man with the gavel names a price and if you're willing to pay that much, you put up your hand or call out."

"I'd love to buy something," Nan said as she eyed the articles on the crowded platform.

Mrs. Bobbsey opened her purse and handed Harry and each of the twins a dollar bill.

"You may each bid up to this amount," she said, "on anything you want."

"Thank you, Mommy," Flossie said.

The Bobbsey party took their places on folding chairs which had been set up inside the tent. In a short while all the chairs were occupied, and some people were standing.

As the auctioneer began his opening speech Nan whispered to Aunt Sarah, "What is it that you meant we'd want to buy?"

Aunt Sarah smiled. "It's still a secret."

The auctioneer pounded his gavel on the stand and the sale began. "The first lot I have," he called, "is a doll's china tea set." He displayed the gaily-decorated cups and saucers, a tea pot and a cream pitcher. "I'll have to sell these 'as is,'" he said. "The set is complete except for a saucer and the sugar bowl. Now, who'll start the bidding at two dollars?"

There was silence. Flossie leaned over to her mother. "Oh, I'd love to have that tea set," she said. "And I don't care if the sugar bowl's missing—all my dollies are sweet enough already!"

The auctioneer went on, "Only two dollars for this lovely tea set, folks—It's worth three times that!"

"I'll bid ten cents!" Flossie piped up.

Everyone laughed and the auctioneer joined in. But still no one else bid.

"Are we going to let this tea set go for only ten cents?" he called out, looking around the room. "Very well, Going for ten cents . . . Going for ten cents. SOLD to the little lady for one thin dime!"

Flossie ran up the aisle and came back proudly holding the set of doll dishes.

"Here's something for the little gentleman!" the auctioneer said, holding up a large decorated cup. "What am I bid for this mustache cup!"

A wave of laughter spread over the audience. Uncle Daniel explained to Freddie that a mustache cup was made with a partition across the opening so that a man's mustache would not get wet while he was drinking from it.

Freddie giggled. "I don't need it now, but I might have a mustache when I'm bigger. I'll bid ten cents!" he shouted.

Little Roy Holden who was seated near the Bobbseys raised his hand. "I'll bid fifteen cents!"

"Fifteen cents," the auctioneer cried. "I hear fifteen cents . . . Do I hear twenty-five?"

"Twenty-five cents!" Freddie burst out.

"Twenty-five cents I have. Do I hear thirty?" the man called, looking at Roy.

Roy shook his head.

The auctioneer's voice rang out, "Going, going, GONE for twenty-five cents!" he cried.

Freddie ran up to get his mustache cup and returned grinning from ear to ear.

Several pieces of furniture were displayed and were sold after spirited bidding.

"We still haven't bought anything, Sis," Bert remarked.

Nan nodded. "And Aunt Sarah's mysterious object hasn't come up for bidding."

The next article the auctioneer held up was an old-fashioned record player with a large horn attached. "Say, that's keen!" Bert exclaimed. "Freddie and I could keep it in our bedroom!" So he bid on the machine and finally it became his for seventy-five cents.

"I know what I want," Nan said. "See that old doll propped up in the chair? It would be wonderful for my collection!" She indicated a cloth doll in a faded silk dress. Its delicate face was made of china.

In a few minutes the doll was brought to the platform. The bidding started at twenty-five cents. Several people seemed to be interested, but Nan kept bidding and it was sold to her for one dollar.

"Harry's the only one who hasn't bought anything," Flossie announced.

Next the auctioneer held up a long, wooden fork with three rounded prongs. "This is an old haying fork," he announced. "Who'll start the bidding at one dollar?"

There was a ripple of laughter in the tent.

"Just what I've always needed," Mrs. Bobbsey whispered jokingly.

"Do I hear fifty cents?" came the voice again. "Fifty cents for this haying fork?"

Suddenly Harry called out, "I'll give you twenty-five cents for it!" The twins exchanged looks of surprise.

"SOLD for twenty-five cents!" the auctioneer cried in relief.

"What are you going to do with a haying fork?" Bert asked, as Harry examined his bargain.

Harry laughed. "Who knows? I guess I can always stand it in a corner and use it for a hat rack!" The children giggled at their cousin's joke.

The auctioneer stepped down from the platform for a little rest and the tent began to buzz with conversation.

"Now he'll put up the more expensive items," a woman next to Nan told her.

At that moment the auctioneer resumed his place. "Ladies and gentlemen," he announced, pounding his gavel for attention, "the next article which I shall put up for bidding is something special. I'm sure everyone in the audience who has children will be interested."

Nan looked expectantly at Aunt Sarah. "Is this it?" she asked excitedly.

Her aunt nodded.

There was a stir in the tent as a man led up to the front of the platform a sturdy brown-and-white Shetland pony. He was harnessed to a basket cart.

"Oh! Isn't he darling?" Flossie squealed.

The other children in the tent thought so too, and they cried out in delight.

"Who will start the bidding at twenty-five

dollars?" the auctioneer called. "Twenty-five dollars for this fine pony and cart!"

After some hesitation Mrs. Bobbsey raised her hand. "Twenty dollars!" she called. Then a voice from the other side of the tent called out, "Twenty-five!"

"Twenty-five dollars, twenty-five dollars! Do I hear thirty?"

Again Mrs. Bobbsey raised her hand. But the other bidder quickly jumped the bid. "Forty dollars!"

So the bidding went, with the other person going five or ten dollars higher each time Mrs. Bobbsey raised her hand. Finally she shook her head. "That's as high as Dick wanted me to go," she whispered to Uncle Daniel.

Then she noticed the disappointed faces of the twins.

"Fifty-five dollars I have," the auctioneer cried. "Going, going . . ."

"Sixty dollars!" Mrs. Bobbsey quickly called out.

The twins held their breath.

"Sixty dollars I hear!" the man cried. "Going for sixty. Going for sixty. GONE for sixty dollars!"

"Wow," Freddie cried, beaming at his mother.

"Goody, goody!" Flossie jumped up and

down and clapped her hands. "May we take him home now?"

While Uncle Daniel took the money and went up to pay the auctioneer, Mrs. Bobbsey explained to the twins that when Aunt Sarah had written that the pony and cart were to be put up for sale, their father had decided to buy them for the children.

"But," she continued, "ponies and carts are not allowed on the streets of Lakeport. So your father and I thought we would leave them here at Meadowbrook. You can use them whenever you come to visit and Harry can enjoy the pony and cart all year."

The twins thought this a good idea. Uncle Daniel came back to report, "The pony's name is Rocket and he's waiting for you outside. Who will drive him back?"

"May Nan and I try?" Bert asked eagerly.

"Very well," Mrs. Bobbsey agreed. "Don't go too fast. We'll ride ahead with Uncle Daniel and meet you at the farm."

After the others had driven off, Bert and Nan, feeling very proud, climbed into the pony cart. Bert took the reins.

"Giddap, Rocket!" he called. "Let's go!"

The little pony trotted obediently out of town and along the road leading to Meadowbrook Farm.

"Isn't this wonderful?" Nan cried. "With Rocket we'll be able to ride all around the country by ourselves."

"Terrific!"

Just then Rocket turned into a lane leading to a small farmhouse. Although Bert pulled firmly on the reins the little pony paid no attention. He trotted into a barn and stopped.

In vain Bert tried to back him out. Rocket stood still.

"Where do you suppose we are, Bert?" Nan asked nervously, looking around.

At that moment an elderly man came into the barn. "Hello, Rocket," he said. "What are you doing here?"

"Why, you're Mr. Burns, aren't you?" Bert asked in surprise. "Is this your barn?"

"Yes and you're Dan Bobbsey's nephew and niece!" the farmer exclaimed. "Did you buy Rocket at the auction?"

Bert explained that he and his sister were just driving the pony home after their mother had purchased him.

"Rocket used to belong to my grandchildren," Mr. Burns told them. "But they've moved away so I put the pony and cart up for sale. I guess Rocket doesn't realize this isn't his home anymore!"

The friendly farmer took hold of Rocket's

bridle and turned him around. He gave him a little slap on the flank and the pony trotted obediently down the lane.

"Thank you, Mr. Burns," Nan called back. "We'll bring Rocket to visit you again."

A little later when Bert turned Rocket up the Bobbsey driveway, Harry ran toward them. The twins could see their cousin was upset.

"What's the matter?" Bert called to him.

"Major, our bull, has been stolen!" Harry cried.

CHAPTER VI

A LOST PICNICKER

"MAJOR gone!" Bert exclaimed. "When did it happen?"

Harry explained that he had fed the prize bull that morning and left him in his pen. "When we got back from the auction I went out to see him and he wasn't there!"

"Did Dinah or Martha notice any strangers around?" Nan asked.

Harry shook his head. "They were busy in the kitchen fixing things for the picnic and didn't hear anything unusual. Dad is talking to the State Troopers on the phone now."

"That's terrible, Harry!" Nan said sympathetically. "Another mystery to solve! We'll help."

"I hope you can solve this one," Harry said sadly. "Major is very valuable!"

Officers Kent and Bennett arrived in a little

while and the children watched in fascination as they tried to figure out what had happened.

"I'd say a truck came up here through the field back of the barn and carried the bull away," Lieutenant Kent told them. "That's why no one at the house heard it."

"Are these the thief's shoe marks?" Bert asked, pointing to some which ran alongside those of the bull out to the field.

The officer nodded. "I suppose the bull was driven up a ramp into the truck."

"Maybe this is a clue to the man who took him," Nan said excitedly. She had picked up a pocket notebook with the initials CM on it. Nothing was written on the inside pages.

"It very well could be," the lieutenant said. "I'll take the notebook along anyway."

Presently the officers went off. That evening the twins waited hopefully for good news from the police, but none came.

Early the next morning Bert ran out to the barn to feed Rocket. He paused to look at Major's empty pen and thought, "It's a shame! Losing the bull is a big blow to Uncle Daniel."

Bert went on. He found the little brown-and-white pony standing quietly in his stall.

"How are you, old fellow?" Bert asked, patting him on the flank.

In answer Rocket put out his nose and nuzzled

Bert. The boy speared some hay into the box and the little animal began to munch hungrily.

As Bert stood watching him, he thought he heard a rustle in the mow above him. Glancing up he was just in time to see a tousled yellow head draw back.

"Who's up there?" Bert called.

"It's just me," came a small voice.

"Well, come down here, whoever you are," Bert said sternly.

A little boy climbed slowly down the ladder. He was about Freddie's age and had yellow hair and big brown eyes. His clothes were rumpled and bits of straw stuck out of his hair.

"Who are you? Where did you come from?" Bert asked in surprise.

"My name is Skipper Brooks. The bus went off without me," the child replied. Then he added, "I'm hungry!"

"I'll take you into the house and give you some breakfast," Bert promised. "Then you can tell us what happened."

Skipper put his hand in Bert's and trotted along by his side. They went upstairs, where Skipper washed, and brushed his hair. Then they came down to the dining room. Everyone looked up from the table in astonishment.

"This is Skipper Brooks," Bert introduced the boy. "I found him in the haymow."

Aunt Sarah motioned Skipper to a chair beside her. "Sit here, dear, and have some breakfast," she said kindly. "Then you can tell us all about your adventure."

Martha put a big bowl of oatmeal before the little boy, and he began to eat hungrily. Freddie and Flossie watched him intently. Skipper finally put down his spoon and reached for his glass of milk. "Where do you live?" Flossie asked him.

"New York," Skipper replied. "But I was on my way to camp when I got off the bus."

Uncle Daniel looked up. "Were you going to the Fresh Air Camp, Sonny?" he inquired.

Skipper nodded. "Yes. But the bus had something the matter with it. The driver stopped to get it fixed and I went down under the bridge to look at the pretty water. Then when I climbed back up to the road, the bus was gone!"

"How did you get here?" Nan asked.

"I walked. I didn't see anybody around this place. I was awful tired so I climbed up onto that shelf with the nice dry grass and went to sleep."

Flossie giggled when she heard Skipper call the haymow a shelf. But Mrs. Bobbsey shook her head warningly for her to stop.

Uncle Daniel pushed back his chair. "I'd better call Mrs. Manily, the camp director, and tell her we have one of her guests with us. She's probably worried about what happened to him!" Daniel Bobbsey was on the committee which ran the Fresh Air Camp for city children every summer.

While he was gone, Freddie and Flossie made friends with Skipper. "We'll take you riding in our new pony cart," Freddie promised.

In a few minutes Uncle Daniel returned. "Mrs. Manily was very glad to learn that you're safe, Skipper. She also said you could come with us to the picnic we're having today."

"That's super!" Harry exclaimed. "You'll have a good time, Skipper. I'm going to take my homing pigeons along and I'll show you how they carry messages!"

Skipper looked a little puzzled but very happy. After church Uncle Daniel harnessed Billy and Betty to the old wagon filled with sweet-smelling hay. The Bobbsey children and Skipper climbed in. Uncle Daniel kept the cage with the pigeons in it on the seat near him.

The first stop was at the Holden farm where Tom and his little brother Roy joined the group. Then they turned into the Stout farm. Bud Stout was a little like his last name.

When he came out of the house he looked embarrassed. "Mark Teron is here," Bud said. "Is it all right for him to come, too?"

Harry made a face. Mark was sort of a bully. But Uncle Daniel said cordially, "Of course. The more the merrier!"

Two more stops added Patty Manners and Kim Harold to the group. It was a beautiful day and the children had a good time singing and joking as Billy and Betty jogged along.

After the hayriders had been on the road for a little while, Bud called out, "May we stop at the spring for a drink of water, Mr. Bobbsey?"

"Sure!" Uncle Daniel pulled the horses off the road. From the side of the hill a stream of

cold water poured down. It fell into a round basin built of stones.

There were no cups, so the children took turns bending over and holding their mouths under the clear stream of water. Mark Teron stood back talking to Bud.

"Bert Bobbsey thinks he's smart because he comes from the city," Mark complained. "I don't like him."

"He seems all right to me," Bud replied.

Mark waited until it was Bert's turn to drink. Then as the Bobbsey boy bent over, Mark stepped up behind him. The next thing Bert knew his face was being pushed into the basin and held there.

He struggled to raise his head but could not do it. His mouth and nose filled with water. Bert held his breath, though. Just when he felt as if his lungs would burst, the grip relaxed.

Gasping for breath, Bert straightened up. He saw Harry punch Mark in the shoulder. "What's the big idea?" Harry cried. "You leave my cousin alone!"

"I didn't hurt the big sissy!" Mark spluttered, aiming a blow at Harry.

"Stop your fighting, you two!" Uncle Daniel ordered. "Mark, if you can't behave yourself, you'll have to walk home!"

Grumbling, Mark followed the others back to

the wagon and climbed in. Everyone talked at once to cover up the unpleasant incident. Soon Uncle Daniel turned into a narrow road which wound through a woods.

"Whoa, Betty! Whoa, Billy!" he called a few minutes later when he reached an open space surrounded by tall pine trees. He turned around in his seat and spoke to the boys and girls in the wagon. "This looks like a good picnic spot. We'll stop here."

There was a lot of laughing and teasing as the children jumped down from the hay wagon. The boys carried the baskets of food to the clearing while Uncle Daniel unhitched the horses.

Bert and Harry spread out the long picnic cloth on the pine needles and anchored each corner with a large stone. Patty and Kim put paper plates and cups around, then went to help Nan and Flossie unpack the baskets of food.

"Ooh! Everything looks good!" Flossie exclaimed, and the others agreed with her.

There were big platters of crisp fried chicken. Next came two blue bowls filled with creamy potato salad, packages of thin bread and butter sandwiches, potato chips, deviled eggs, pickles, olives, and crisp celery stuffed with cheese. There was also a bowl of cole slaw decorated with slices of pimiento.

Freddie had been watching the unpacking, his

blue eyes growing wider by the minute. "Oh boy!" he cried. "This is the best-looking picnic I ever went to!"

Last, Nan and Patty lifted out two cakes—one covered with fluffy coconut and the other with shiny dark chocolate. "I can hardly wait for dessert!" Flossie declared.

Little Skipper's eyes were big as saucers. "I'm glad I did get lost," he said.

Some of the children had scattered and were playing among the trees. When Nan announced that the picnic was ready, Uncle Daniel took a whistle from his pocket and blew a shrill blast.

"Food's on!" he called. "Come and get it!"

Quickly the boys and girls took their places around the picnic cloth. Bert and Harry poured cold milk from three big thermoses into paper cups.

With many ohs and ahs the children began to eat. Finally Freddie stood up. "I'm awf'ly sorry," he said regretfully, "but I just can't finish my cake!"

"Put it here," Uncle Daniel remarked. "I'll eat it."

Hearing this, Flossie passed him her cake, too. Then, when he was looking the other way, Nan giggled and slid the rest of her piece onto her uncle's plate.

When Uncle Daniel looked at the pile of cake

he laughed and all the others joined in. "Goodness!" he exclaimed. "If I eat all this, I'll look like Santa Claus!"

Everyone got up from the picnic spot and stretched. "Let's have a game of hide and seek," Nan proposed. "I'll be 'it' first."

Nan covered her eyes and the boys and girls disappeared among the trees. She caught Patty first as she spotted the girl's head over a low bush. Soon the others were dashing about trying to get "home free."

"Where's Flossie?" Nan asked when everyone else had been brought in.

"She's still hiding, I guess," Roy ventured. He had started out with Flossie but lost sight of her when he ran in.

"Flossie!" Nan called. "Come on in!"

But Flossie did not appear. All the children called and called and Uncle Daniel blew his whistle, but Flossie did not answer.

"Where do you suppose she can be?" Nan said worriedly.

Little Skipper spoke up timidly. "I think she went that way." He pointed off among the trees.

Harry heard him. "The cliff's over there!" he exclaimed. "We'd better go after Flossie before she falls down on the rocks!"

CHAPTER VII

A ROCKY TRAP

NAN turned pale. "A cliff!" she cried, and dashed off through the woods, with Bert and Harry close behind her.

The trio soon reached the edge of the cliff. "Oh!" Nan gasped. "Look!"

"Flossie!" Bert and Harry chorused. They stared unbelievingly down over the cliff.

There, by herself among a pile of rocks, was Flossie! She was crying.

"Come back! Climb up!" Nan cried.

"I can't. The stones are too roll-y."

"She's right," said Bert. "We'll have to make a chain by holding hands."

He grabbed Harry's right wrist and Harry clasped his, Nan took her cousin's left. Bud held her other wrist, then the girls joined the line. Mark Teron stood to one side, not offering to help.

"I hurt my arm yesterday," he used as an excuse.

Uncle Daniel ran up as the line started to move down the cliff, and said he would act as "anchor man" at the end of the "human rope." In a short while Bert reached Flossie and put his free arm around her shoulders.

Not a word was spoken until the little girl had been rescued. Then Nan said, "Oh, Flossie, why did you run off and scare us all?"

"I wanted to hide in a good place," her little sister explained. "I thought I'd just go down this big hill a little way, but I couldn't stop, and I slid and slid."

Uncle Daniel patted her, then said with a chuckle, "You're lucky you didn't slide to the bottom of this rocky cliff, or there'd have been only one-half of a certain Flossie Bobbsey." He became serious. "The State ought to put up a fence here. It's entirely too dangerous."

"If they don't," said Harry, "why don't all of us get together and do it?"

"All right. We will," his father agreed.

The group walked back to the picnic spot. Presently Harry said, "It's time to let the pigeons loose!" He ran to the hay wagon where the cage with the carrier pigeons had been left.

"What are you going to write the message on?" Tom wanted to know.

Uncle Daniel took a small notebook from his pocket. "Here, son, use this," he said, tearing out a sheet of paper and handing it to Harry.

While everyone was intently watching Harry print a message, Mark Teron sidled over to the cage. Quietly he opened the door and one of the pigeons flew out!

Bert turned around just in time to see this. Quick as a flash he ran over and caught the second pigeon as it was about to fly away.

"That was a mean trick!" he cried, putting the bird back into the cage and fastening the lock.

"Oh, will the pigeon get lost?" Flossie asked fearfully.

"No," Uncle Daniel said. "It'll just go home."

"You think you're smart, Bert Bobbsey!" Mark was muttering. He gave the boy a shove which almost knocked him off his feet.

"Here, here, none of that!" Uncle Daniel exclaimed. "You two boys had better have a wrestling match fair and square, and get this out of your systems!"

"I'm game!" Bert declared, and Mark nodded.

The other children formed a circle as Bert and Mark grabbed each other. Mark was heavier than Bert and soon had the Bobbsey boy on the ground. But Bert had learned wrestling at school and in a few minutes was forcing Mark's shoulders to the dirt.

"Come on, Bert!" Harry cried. "Pin him!"

Mark struggled but suddenly both his shoulders hit the ground. Bert stood up immediately. He had won!

"Come on," he urged. "Let's send off the carrier pigeon!"

While Mark got sullenly to his feet, Harry put the little roll of paper into a tiny metal tube. Fastened to this was a band which he pinched into place around one of the bird's legs.

"What does the message say?" Freddie asked.

Harry grinned. "It's to Martha and Dinah and says we'll be home to supper at six."

Then he took the pigeon in both hands and with a little toss sent it on its way. In a few seconds the bird was high in the sky. It circled several times, then started for the farm.

"I wish I could fly like that!" Freddie observed, as the carrier pigeon disappeared.

"Now for some games," Uncle Daniel said. "You older boys hunt for fallen, but not rotted, tree limbs we can use to build that rail fence at the cliff. Don't go far. I'll play with the girls."

The boys scattered to look for the limbs. Bert and Harry stayed together. They found several, then the farm boy said, "Bert, how would you like to see the quarry?"

Bert nodded eagerly. Unnoticed by the others, the two boys hurried off among the trees. Soon they reached the huge hole in the ground.

"This limestone was used for building around here," Harry explained, "but the quarry hasn't been worked for a long time."

The two boys stood at the edge of the excavation and looked down. The jagged layers of rock reached far below the surface of the ground.

"Can we climb down?" Bert asked eagerly.

Harry looked around. "Say!" he exclaimed. "There's a ladder. Let's try it."

The cousins ran to it and started down. They found that the ladder covered only the sheer upper portion of the excavation and then ended. At this point the slope was more gradual, and Bert and Harry were able to gain a footing.

"We can climb down from here to the bottom," Bert said. "It'll be easy."

"Sure," Harry agreed, beginning to scramble over the dusty rock.

Together the boys made their way to the bottom of the huge hole in the ground. There they discovered a pool of water and amused themselves by tossing pieces of rock into it.

"Boy, it must be deep!" Bert remarked. "You can't see the bottom!"

After a while Harry suggested that they go back. "Dad will be wondering where we are."

As they reached the sheer part of the quarry, Bert was in the lead. "Isn't this the spot we came down the ladder?" he called back to his cousin.

"Yes. What's the matter?"

"The ladder's gone! We'll never be able to climb out!"

Harry hurried to Bert's side. "Maybe it was a little farther to the right," he said.

But though the boys looked along the rock face in both directions, there was no sign of the ladder.

"Someone pulled it up!" Harry said. "I'll bet it was Mark! He was angry when you beat him at wrestling and he's trying to get even!"

"I suppose he's laughing at us right now," Bert said. "I wish we could get out anyway. Then the laugh would be on him!"

But, try as they might, the boys could not get up to the rim of the quarry.

"I guess we're stuck!" Harry said in despair.

"Let's go back to the bottom and look around there," Bert suggested.

So, slipping and sliding, the two boys made their way down again. The sun was lower in the sky by now and the bottom of the pit was in deep shadow. The boys walked around, carefully skirting the deep pool, and looking for a way out of their rocky prison.

In the meantime, back at the picnic grove, the other boys had come in and joined a ball game which the girls had organized. The small children were kept busy chasing the ball while the older ones took turns at bat.

Finally Uncle Daniel, who had occasionally joined in the game, announced, "It's time to start back. Let's get everything into the wagon."

There was a great scurrying around to gather

up the picnic things. Suddenly Nan said, "Where are Bert and Harry?"

No one answered. "I suppose they're still looking for rails," Uncle Daniel said, "but I'll find them."

"I'll do it," Mark offered, and raced off.

He went straight to the quarry, picked up a ladder lying on the ground, and put it in place down the side.

"I'll pretend I don't know anything about it," the boy told himself, chuckling.

Mark had just succeeded in replacing the ladder when Uncle Daniel came up beside him. "Do you see the boys?" he asked anxiously.

Mark peered down into the quarry. No one was there!

"Why—why—" he stammered. "What could have happened to them?" Mark was so frightened that his knees shook.

At this moment, someone clapped him on the shoulder. He turned around with a start. It was Harry!

"You thought you had us trapped in the quarry, didn't you?" Harry asked angrily.

"And you would have if we hadn't found another way out!" Bert joined in.

"Wh-what did you do?" Mark asked.

Harry explained that Bert had found a rough path up on the opposite side of the excavation and the boys had managed to scramble out that way. They had then worked their way through the underbrush to the spot where they now were.

"That's the third mean trick you've played today," Bert said, advancing on Mark with his fist clenched.

Uncle Daniel spoke up. "Did you really pull that ladder up, Mark?" he asked sternly.

Mark hung his head. "I'm sorry," he muttered. "I just wanted to scare the fellows. I wasn't going to leave them down there!" Then he added to Harry, "But you really scared me. I thought something terrible had happened when I didn't see you in the quarry!"

"In that case, Mark, perhaps you've been punished enough," Uncle Daniel observed. "But if you're going to play with these boys, you'll have to learn to behave yourself!"

Mark promised, so nothing was said of the incident when they joined the others. The rail fence was laid at the edge of the cliff, then they all went to the hay wagon.

As they settled down for the long ride home, Flossie said, "Skipper, did you have a good time?"

"Yes." Skipper sighed. "It was the best day I ever had in my whole life!"

"You'll have to come visit us again while

you're at the Fresh Air Camp," Uncle Daniel said kindly.

"Yes," Freddie agreed. "So you can go for that ride in our pony cart."

"And you can help us solve our mysteries," Flossie added.

"What mysteries?" Kim Harold asked. "I didn't know there were any mysteries about Meadowbrook Farm!"

"Somebody plays our piano in the middle of the night," Flossie said.

"Oh!"

"And our prize bull Major was stolen while we were at the auction yesterday," Harry added.

"How terrible!" Kim exclaimed.

Skipper sat up, his brown eyes snapping with excitement. "Was the bull in the same barn where you found me?" he asked.

"Why yes, Skipper," Bert remarked. "Did you see him?"

The little boy explained that when he had gone into the barn he had heard an animal snorting and pawing at the floor but he had been too frightened to go near the stall.

"I just climbed the ladder and went to sleep in the hay," he said. "But I woke up and heard two men talking about the bull. I thought they were the people who lived on the farm and I didn't want them to find me. So I kept very still."

"Did you see the men?" Nan asked eagerly.

The little boy shook his head. "I was too scared to look," he replied, "but I heard them talking about taking the bull away."

"Where?" Bert asked excitedly.

"I don't know."

"Did they call each other by name?" Harry spoke up.

"Yes. They said Mitch and Clint," Skipper replied.

CHAPTER VIII

PRIZE PARADERS

"MITCH and Clint!" Harry looked at his father in bewilderment. "Do you know any men around here with those names, Dad?" he asked.

Uncle Daniel shook his head. "Not in this neighborhood, nor anywhere. But as soon as we get home, I'll report to the State Troopers what Skipper said."

"Now maybe we'll get Major back soon," Harry said hopefully. "Oh, I want to so much. Besides, he's entered in the County Fair and I'm sure he'll get an award."

First Harry's friends were dropped at their homes. Then Uncle Daniel drove to the Fresh Air Camp and turned in at the gate. In a few minutes they came to a cluster of tents surrounding a large log cabin on the banks of the river.

"Say, this looks great!" Freddie exclaimed and grinned at Skipper. "I'd like to stay here, too!"

As Uncle Daniel stopped the horses, a pleasant-looking woman came out of the log cabin and walked toward them.

"Good afternoon, Mrs. Manily," Uncle Daniel called. "We've brought your missing guest!"

"I'm very glad to have him here," the woman said kindly, reaching up to help Skipper down from the hay wagon. "I hope he'll be happy with us."

"I'm sure he will be," said Mr. Bobbsey.

"See you soon," the children chorused as they waved good-by to Skipper.

After the little boy had run into the cabin, Mrs. Manily sighed and said, "I do want him to have a good time here. His father died last year and his mother is an invalid. There is no money for Skipper to have anything but just necessities."

"Perhaps we can help him in some way," Nan said kindly.

"You have helped by taking him on your picnic," the camp director assured her, waving good-by.

When the Bobbseys reached the farm they found that both homing pigeons had returned and Martha had received the carrier message.

No word had been heard from the police about Major. Uncle Daniel called headquarters and told the trooper who answered what Skipper had overheard.

"That may turn out to be a good lead," the man replied. "We'll let you know if we come across anything."

The next morning at breakfast Aunt Sarah reminded the twins that their father would arrive late that afternoon.

"Goody!" Flossie cried. "He'll be here for the Fourth of July!"

"That's right," Nan agreed. "Tomorrow is the Fourth. We ought to plan some sort of celebration."

"There are to be speeches and a band concert on the village green at eleven o'clock," Uncle Daniel said.

"We could have a parade beforehand," Bert suggested.

"That would be fun!" Flossie clapped her hands. "We can dress up!"

"And march into town," Harry said.

He went to the telephone and called Patty, Kim, Tom, and Bud. They eagerly agreed to take part in the parade, and to come over to the farm and make plans.

As soon as everyone was gathered on the front porch, Nan asked, "What shall we wear?"

"We could make red-white-and-blue paper hats," Patty suggested.

"That's a good idea," Nan agreed. "I'll see if Aunt Sarah has any crepe paper."

In a few minutes she returned carrying several rolls of brightly colored paper. "We're lucky," she said. "It's just what we want!"

They set to work and soon had seven hats pasted together. The older boys made theirs three-sided. "We'll all look like George Washington!" Bert chuckled, putting on his tricorn.

"I want to be Uncle Sam!" Freddie insisted.

"All right," Nan said. "We'll make you a top hat and you can wear those red-and-white striped pajamas you brought!"

"I want to be somebody special, too!" Flossie spoke up.

"You could be Miss Liberty," Kim remarked.

"What will I wear?" Flossie asked doubtfully.

Nan thought a moment, then said, "You can have a crown of gold paper, and wear a white nightgown!"

"Nan, you should ride Rocket with Freddie and Flossie standing up in the cart!" Harry suggested. "It'll be like a float."

"Wonderful!" she exclaimed.

"I have an idea for us fellows," Bud put in.

"Let's decorate our bicycles with the paper and have a race after the parade."

"That would be great!" Harry agreed.

By the time the twins' mother was ready to leave for the station to meet their father, all the costumes had been assembled and the plans completed. The children agreed to meet at the farm by ten o'clock the following morning.

"Oh, Daddy!" cried Flossie as Mr. Bobbsey stepped from the train, "we're going to have the most bee-yoo-ti-ful Fourth of July parade tomorrow!"

Then Nan told him about the purchase of Rocket. "He's just the most precious pet!" she said, hugging her father. "Thank you for letting us buy her."

The twins took turns telling Mr. Bobbsey all that had happened since their arrival.

"You really have been busy since I saw you last!" he said, "and I'm sorry about Major."

The next morning Patty and Kim arrived wearing shorts and blouses. Nan was dressed the same way. The older boys had on neat blue jeans and white shirts.

Flossie looked very sweet in her white nightgown with the gold crown on her yellow curls. Freddie strutted about with his tall red-white-and-blue hat and the striped pajamas.

"Nan, you'd better start on in the cart with Freddie and Flossie," Aunt Sarah advised. "I'll drive the other girls and the boys with their bicycles to the edge of town. You can parade to the green from there."

Soon they all met and began the march. Word of the little parade spread. Boys and girls and some parents began to line the sidewalks to watch. Nan on Rocket and Freddie and Flossie in the cart drew lots of applause.

"Aren't they sweet?"

"What a splendid idea!"

"Very good!"

The children glowed with pleasure as they marched to the village green. The mayor greeted them and handed Nan a tall candy Uncle Sam.

"We wanted your 'float' to have a special prize," he said, smiling. "That was a clever idea, Uncle Sam and Miss Liberty."

A few moments later Uncle Daniel picked up the boys and drove them and their bicycles to the end of Main Street. They quickly unloaded the machines and took their places.

Harry, Bud, and Tom had called several friends the night before and urged them to join the race. Twelve boys were lined up.

"The police are clearing Main Street for you all the way to the grandstand," Uncle Daniel said.

Although Main Street was fairly wide, the row of boys took up its entire width. Quickly the town policeman cleared the street of all traffic.

"Let's go!" Tom shouted as Mr. Bobbsey sounded the whistle.

It was about half a mile from the starting place to the village green. The boys bent over the handle bars and their feet flashed up and down as they pedaled furiously.

Tom and Bert took an early lead. Bud came puffing along in third place. But as he looked over his shoulder to see who was behind him, his wheel turned out of control. The next minute he was sprawled in the middle of the street!

"Watch out!" Harry yelled as he managed to swing around his fallen friend.

The next boy was not so lucky. He ran into Bud's bicycle and landed on the ground nearby. In a few minutes there were five boys in the pile-up! By the time they got to their feet and onto their bicycles again, the others were far up the street.

"I'm coming!" Harry shouted as he drew abreast of Bert and Tom.

Bert grinned as his cousin pedaled past him across the finish line. "Good work, Harry!" he called.

"Harry Bobbsey is the winner!" the mayor announced.

The crowd cheered, then everybody took seats on the grass to hear the program which had been arranged. The mayor read the Declaration of Independence and the Fire House band played several patriotic songs.

At the end of the exercises, when everybody stood up to sing *The Star Spangled Banner,* the mayor came to the edge of the platform.

"Before you leave our beautiful town," he boomed over the loud-speaker, "I have an important announcement to make."

"I wonder what it is," Nan whispered to her twin.

Everyone listened intently. The mayor explained that in the afternoon a plane would fly over the area of Meadowbrook and a stunt man would parachute onto one of the neighboring farms.

"We don't know which farm this will be," he continued, "but the first person reaching the parachutist after he lands will receive a prize!"

A buzz of excitement swept over the crowd. There were many farms in the area and everyone wondered which would be the lucky one.

After the meeting broke up, Aunt Sarah said, "I'm inviting all the paraders to come back to Meadowbrook Farm to lunch. We can watch for the parachutist from there."

It was decided that the girls would go back in the pony cart while the grownups and the boys rode in the station wagon.

"I hope everything's all right at the farm," Harry observed. "The last time we were away, Major was stolen!"

"Speaking of Major," Uncle Daniel said, "I asked all the farmers at the ceremonies if they had any clues to his disappearance. They knew nothing about our bull, but they did say that several valuable animals had also been stolen from them during the past few weeks."

"Probably by Mitch and Clint!" Bert declared.

By this time they had reached the farm. The boys ran quickly to a picnic table which Martha and Dinah had set up on the lawn.

"Oh boy, does that look good!" Bud cried. "I hope the girls come soon so we can eat!"

Rocket turned into the lane not long afterward and soon the children and grownups were enjoying the delicious lunch. They discussed the parade and bicycle race.

"I'm sure sorry I broke up the race!" Bud said. "I just looked around and the next thing I knew I was on the ground!"

Nan giggled. "It was funny to see you all rolling around in the street! But," she added, "I'm glad no one was hurt!"

"And everyone knew Freddie and I were Uncle Sam and Miss Liberty!" Flossie put in proudly. "I heard one lady say she thought we were awf'ly good!"

Then Tom spoke up. "I wonder what time that plane was to fly over?"

"I think I hear one now!" Freddie exclaimed, jumping up from the table.

They all listened. Sure enough, they could hear the drone of an airplane off in the distance.

"Let's go out in the pasture," Harry proposed. "We can see better from there."

The children dashed out to the meadow. Shielding their eyes from the sun with their hands, they gazed up to the sky. The plane, which a moment before had been only a speck, could now be seen clearly.

It passed directly over the watching children, then turned to the east.

"It's going away!" Flossie cried, disappointed.

"But look! It's coming back!" Freddie shouted.

The plane circled once more. Then something dropped from it. In another second a white parachute billowed out and began to float toward the ground.

"It's the parachutist and he's coming this way!" Bert cried.

CHAPTER IX

"WHOA, THERE! WHOA!"

BREATHLESSLY the children watched the man swinging at the end of the long rope attached to the parachute. He appeared to be heading toward the Bobbsey farm.

Then a little gust of wind came and blew the parachutist to the left. "He's coming down on our farm!" Tom Holden yelled. He dashed across the pasture to the fence which separated the two properties.

"Wait, Tom!" Bert called after him. "I think he'll land here after all!"

Tom paused, uncertain, as the wind changed again. This time the parachute was blown directly over the Bobbsey orchard. It was wafted lower and lower.

"I think the man's going to land in a tree!" Nan said excitedly.

As she spoke the white parachute settled over several trees and hung there, limp. All the chil-

Bert quickly freed the man

dren raced across the meadow and into the orchard. Dodging in and out among the trees, they made for the parachute.

As Bert was running under a particularly tall tree he heard someone call, "Here I am! Help me get down!"

Bert peered up through the leafy branches. There, almost at the top of the tree, was the stunt man. The lines of his parachute seemed to be caught and he could not move.

"I'll be right there!" Bert assured him. Nimbly he began to climb the tree.

"Just unfasten these lines from my belt," the man directed when Bert got to him. "I can't reach them."

Bert quickly freed the man. "Oh thank you," he said. The two climbed down the tree. The other children waited at the foot of the tree, starry-eyed.

The parachutist jumped to the ground. "Well," he said, laughing, "I guess this young man here wins the prize. He even climbed a tree to rescue me!"

As they all waited expectantly, the stunt man pulled an envelope from his pocket and handed it to Bert.

"What is it?" Freddie asked impatiently.

"Open it quick!" Flossie urged.

Bert tore open the envelope and pulled out a

sheet of paper. A smile came over his face. "It's an order to buy something at the Meadowbrook Sports Shop," he explained. "I can get anything I want there as a gift."

"Say, that's great," Harry said. "What'll you pick out?"

"I know!" Flossie spoke up. "You can buy a bed for Snoop!"

"But we already made Snoop a bed," Bert protested, "out of an old carton."

"Snoop doesn't like that one," Freddie put in. "He won't sleep in it."

Bert promised to think over the matter, then asked the stunt man about his parachute.

"I'd certainly appreciate it if you boys would help me get it out of the tree," the parachutist said.

The four older boys set to work untangling the parachute lines from the tree top and finally were able to lift the huge nylon bag free. They carried it to the meadow, laid it on the grass, and folded the cloth as best they could.

"Very good job," its owner said.

The grownups had strolled over to examine the parachute. Now Uncle Daniel offered to drive the stunt man into town.

"I'd appreciate that," he said.

Freddie looked down the road a long time after the man had gone. Then he said to his mother and Flossie, "Maybe when I grow up, I'll be a chute man and float through the air."

Mrs. Bobbsey smiled. "Right now, if you want to grow up, you'll eat some supper and go to bed!"

Around midnight, when everyone at the farm was asleep, Nan awakened. Someone was playing the piano again, exactly the way Flossie had described it—just scales!

"It can't be," Nan told herself. "I must be dreaming."

She lay still and listened. There it came again. Someone *was* downstairs and he or she *was* playing the piano! And fancier now!

The notes came in little runs, then there would be a discordant *thump*.

"I'm going to get Uncle Daniel and see who it is," Nan decided.

She slipped on her robe and slippers and knocked at his door. When he came out, she told him in whispers about the strange music. It had stopped now.

He switched on the light. "All right, we'll go down and see who's there," he agreed. "Maybe a sleepwalker."

"Freddie does walk in his sleep sometimes," Nan said. "He usually goes to the kitchen for some milk."

Together Nan and Uncle Daniel crept down

the stairs. When they reached the living room he snapped on the light there. Nobody was at the piano or anywhere in the room. They walked from room to room but found nothing unusual. Snoop was curled up in his box in the kitchen.

Nan was embarrassed but insisted she had heard the piano. "I guess a ghost must have been playing it," she said.

The next morning at breakfast Nan told about the music. "It was probably a mouse," Bert said, grinning.

"Don't be silly," Nan answered. "A mouse isn't heavy enough to push down the keys."

"Well, I hope I'll hear this ghost the next time he visits us," Uncle Daniel said with a chuckle. "Maybe I'll be able to catch him before he gets away."

Nan laughed. "How do you hold onto a ghost?" she asked.

"By his sheet!" Freddie spoke up.

"Oh, you think this is a pretend ghost," Uncle Daniel teased.

"Aren't all ghosts pretend?" Flossie asked.

"Of course."

After breakfast Aunt Sarah said, "How would you children like to help on the farm this morning?"

"Oh yes," Flossie agreed. "May I feed the chickens and gather the eggs?"

"All right. And Freddie can help you." The small twins went off with Uncle Daniel.

Aunt Sarah went on. "Anybody want to help me weed the vegetable garden and plant some seeds for winter carrots and beets?"

"I will," Nan offered.

The boys elected to help clean the stables, put in fresh straw and hay and water.

The children had just finished their work and had met at the picnic table for a little snack when Mark Teron walked into the yard.

"I came to see your pony," he announced. "My dad says he'll buy me one if I'd like to ride it."

"Sure, Mark," Bert replied cordially. "Come out to the barn and I'll introduce you to Rocket."

Harry joined them and the three boys strolled off toward the big white barn. Rocket was in his stall contentedly munching some oats when Bert went in.

"Come on, boy," he said, leading the little pony out into the barnyard. "Someone wants to see you."

The three boys gathered around Rocket, admiring his smooth coat and stroking his white mane.

"Can you ride him?" Mark asked. "Or do you always have to harness him to a cart?"

"Of course not," Bert said. "I haven't ridden

him yet, but I'm sure I could. He's very gentle."

"Let's put a saddle on and try him out," Mark proposed. "We'll draw lots to see who gets the first ride."

They drew straws and Harry won. He ran into the barn and brought out a small saddle. While he went back for some stirrups Mark helped Bert saddle the pony.

"Okay," Mark called when Harry returned.

Harry adjusted the stirrups and mounted. At once Rocket reared into the air and took off like a shot!

"Whoa, Rocket! Whoa!" Harry cried, almost falling off the saddle. "What's the matter with you?"

Harry felt as if he were being shaken to pieces. The boy pulled on the reins with all his might, trying to slow the little animal's pace. But Rocket paid no attention. He dashed out of the barnyard and across the pasture.

Bert and Mark ran after him, yelling, *"Whoa! Whoa!"*

This only made the pony go faster. He headed across the end of the orchard and toward a neighbor's cornfield.

"Oh boy!" Harry thought. "If he runs into Mr. Trimble's corn, there's going to be trouble!"

Mr. Trimble's farm bordered the Bobbseys' for a short distance. He was an unfriendly old bachelor who lived alone in a weatherbeaten farmhouse. His corn was his special pride.

Rocket reached the cornfield and trampled several plants. Then Harry managed to steer him toward a low fence. Faced by the bars, the pony refused to jump. He stopped so suddenly that Harry flew over his head, and landed in a pasture on the other side.

Bert and Mark reached the field just as Harry was painfully picking himself up. "Are you hurt?" Bert asked anxiously.

Harry shook his head. "Just knocked the wind out of me," he said. "But let's get out of this field before old Trimble sees us."

Bert grabbed Rocket by the bridle and led him back to the Bobbsey property. "I can't understand what made Rocket act like that," he said. "It was almost as if—" He stopped and felt under the pony's saddle.

"This was it!" he exclaimed, holding up a burr. "But how did that get there?"

Something about Mark's strange expression made Bert cry out, "Did you put this burr there?"

CHAPTER X

THE UNDERWATER RESCUE

WHEN Bert accused him of putting the burr under Rocket's saddle, Mark started to run away. But Harry was too quick for him. He grabbed Mark by the arm and swung him around.

"I thought you told Dad you'd behave yourself if you played with us," he said sternly. "Bert and I ought to teach you a lesson!"

Mark shook off Harry's hand. "I didn't know Rocket would run away," he whined. "I just wanted to have a little fun! But you never could take a joke! Besides, two against one's no fair."

"It wouldn't have been much of a joke if Harry had been hurt," Bert reminded him.

"And it's not going to be a joke when Mr. Trimble finds his corn broken down," Harry said. "You know how grouchy he is."

"He probably won't even notice it," Mark scoffed, and walked off.

97

But Mr. Trimble did notice the damage and hurried over to the Bobbsey farm that afternoon. With a scowl on his sunburned face, he strode across the barnyard, where Uncle Daniel was repairing a barn lock.

"Where's that scalawag son of yours?" he demanded loudly.

Daniel Bobbsey straightened up. "My son is not a scalawag," he replied calmly. "If you've come about your corn, I'll be glad to pay you for any loss."

"People got no business letting animals run wild on other folks' property," Mr. Trimble replied, still scowling deeply.

"It was an accident," Uncle Daniel explained patiently. "The pony ran away and Harry couldn't stop him."

Harry and Bert had seen Mr. Trimble talking to Uncle Daniel and now joined them. "I'm sorry Rocket and I got into your cornfield," the boy apologized. "Only a few stalks were knocked down."

Mr. Trimble stopped scowling. "Well, maybe I did make too much fuss over the corn," he admitted. "Seems like I've had nothing but trouble ever since I let Mitch and Clint go."

"Mitch and Clint!" Bert and Harry repeated excitedly.

"They were a couple of farmhands I had,"

the neighbor replied. "They were pretty good with my cows, but I couldn't depend on 'em to stay around when I needed 'em. So last week I told the pair to clear out."

Daniel Bobbsey told his neighbor about the loss of Major, the bull, and what little Sandy had overheard. "Have you any idea where Mitch and Clint went?" he concluded.

Mr. Trimble shook his head. "No, I haven't. But if they ever come around again I'll let you know."

"Do you have a picture of them?" Bert asked.

"No, I don't."

"Any sample of their handwriting?"

"No," Mr. Trimble answered. "My goodness, boy, you sound like a detective!"

Bert laughed. "I want to find Major so my cousin can enter him in the County Fair. Can you think of any clue we could give the police?"

Mr. Trimble cupped his chin in hand. "Well, now, this might help a little. Mitch had quite an assortment of big colored handkerchiefs. He always carried a couple with him. Sometimes he wore one around his neck, cowboy style."

"That's a neat clue," said Bert. "Uncle Daniel, may I call State Police Headquarters and tell them?"

"Yes, go ahead."

The two boys hurried to the house and put in

the call. Just as they finished, Tom Holden and Bud Stout arrived. Both boys held fishing poles and Tom had a can of worms.

"We thought maybe you fellows would go fishing with us," Tom proposed.

"How about it, Bert?" Harry asked.

"Sure, I'd like to go. Nan and Flossie and Freddie are going into town with our mothers, so we're on our own."

The two boys ran into the house and chose a couple of rods and a wicker basket for their catch.

"Let's go over to the cove," Harry suggested as they started off. "There's usually pretty good fishing there."

They walked across the fields until they came to the riverbank. Then they made their way upstream to the quiet cove. Finally they sat down on the edge and baited their hooks. When the lines had been thrown into the water, the boys remained very still, waiting for a bite.

Suddenly Bert's line grew taut. "I've hooked something!" he whispered.

Bert jerked up his line with such force that the fish on the end of it swung around and slapped Harry in the face!

"Hey!" Harry yelled. "It's a good fish, but I don't want to kiss it!"

The boys burst into laughter and teased Bert for being a green fisherman.

"I guess I did get a little excited," he admitted. "I'll try not to hit anyone else!" he added with a chuckle, taking his catch off the hook and dropping it into the basket.

Tom had the next bite, and then Harry caught a good-sized bass.

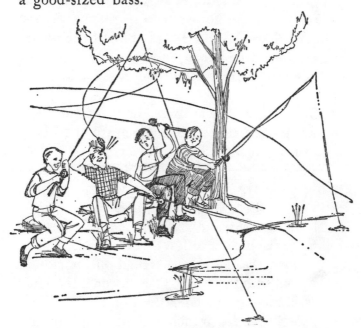

Bud grew discouraged. "I'm going out on that limb," he decided, pointing to a tree whose branches extended over the water.

"You're no bird, Buddy boy," Tom teased his friend. "You're too heavy for that branch!"

"I'll be all right," the stout boy insisted. He climbed into the tree and then inched his way out on the limb. "This is great!" he cried, lying down flat on the narrow limb and dropping his line into the water.

For a while all the boys were quiet. No one spoke as they did not want to frighten away the fish. All that could be heard was a little woodpecker in a tree nearby drilling for insects.

Suddenly there was a loud *crack* and a big splash!

"Bud!" the other three boys yelled. The branch had finally snapped beneath the heavy boy, throwing him into the water!

The three waited for their friend's head to pop up above the surface. Several seconds passed, but there was no sign of Bud.

"He must be caught down there!" Bert exclaimed. "Come on, fellows!"

Instantly the three boys kicked off their shoes and dived into the water to look for him. They found Bud pinned under the branch. His shirt was caught on the branch and was holding him under water!

"We must get him loose!" Bert thought.

The boys had to surface for air. Then they dived under again and managed to pull Bud free. Quickly they came to the top and towed Bud to shore. He was unconscious.

"We'll have to give him artificial respiration!" Bert declared. He had gone to a first-aid class in Lakeport and knew the procedure for mouth-to-mouth resuscitation.

They laid Bud on his back and tilted back his head. Bert kneeled beside him and began his work.

After some time Bud opened his eyes and coughed. "What happened?" he murmured groggily.

Tom told him. "You nearly drowned!"

Bud sat up. "I remember now," he said. "I got stuck on something and couldn't get loose."

Bert explained what had happened.

"Thanks, fellows," the stout boy said gratefully. "You saved my life!" Then he added with a weak grin, "I'm sorry I scared all the fish away!"

"They couldn't compete with a big fish like you!" Tom agreed jokingly. "Anyway, I've had enough fishing for today!"

Bert and Harry felt the same. Bert picked up the wicker basket with the three fish inside. "Here, Bud," he said, "you can have mine. You tried harder than any of us."

Harry and Tom grinned and quickly donated theirs too.

"I didn't hook any fish but I'm going home with three," Bud said with a wan smile.

The boys collected their poles and started the walk back. "Let's keep in the sun," Harry suggested. "Maybe our clothes will dry out by the time we get home."

"That's a good idea," Bert agreed. "We might scare our families if we arrived dripping!"

The four cut through the strip of woods that bordered the water until they reached open fields. Then they started downstream parallel to the river.

Suddenly Bud, who was carrying the basket of fish, noticed he was being followed. The odor of the fish had attracted a large gray cat and four kittens. The meowing mother cat and her kittens walked single file behind the stout boy.

"Bud, how about throwing them one of your fish!" Tom teased.

Bud peered into the basket. "I'll give them the smallest one."

Tom's fish was tossed to the parade of cats. They pounced on it immediately, and the boys hurried on.

As they walked, a movement in the woods on his left attracted Harry's attention. He stopped. "Do you see anything in there, fellows?" he asked in a whisper.

"I hear it," Bert answered. "Sounds like some sort of animal."

"What do you think it is?" Bud asked.

"I don't know, but I'm going to take a look!" Bert said and started to run toward the woods.

The other boys followed. When they caught up with Bert he motioned them to stop. "It's just on the other side of those bushes," he whispered.

Stealthily, he crept forward. Then suddenly he stopped and began to laugh. "It's a cow!" he cried.

Tom ran up. "There's a tag in her ear." He read it. "Why this cow belongs to Mr. Peter Burns. How do you suppose she got over here?"

"I don't know but I'd better return her to him," said Harry.

"I'll go with you," Bert offered.

Tom and Bud decided they would continue to their own homes while Harry and Bert made the detour to the Burns farm.

Harry took hold of the cow's halter and headed off across the field. Bert followed, slapping the animal now and then to help guide her.

Mrs. Burns met the boys as they turned into the lane leading to her farm. "Where did you find Bessie?" she asked in surprise. "She's been missin' since yesterday and my husband was terribly worried. She's one of our best milkers."

Harry explained how they had come across the animal. "Well, thank you both for bringing her home," Mrs. Burns said. "My husband hasn't been feelin' well lately and he's been extra worried over losin' Bessie."

The boys put the cow in her stall in the barn, then hurried on to the Bobbsey farm. As they walked into the kitchen, Dinah greeted them with an astounding announcement.

"I heard that piano ghost! It sure was real. And I got proof somebody was there when everybody was out!"

CHAPTER XI

CHERRY TREE MISHAP

AT DINAH's announcement, all the Bobbsey children gathered to learn the details about the ghostly piano playing.

"You heard it?" Nan queried.

"I sure did, honey. Nobody else was in the house, so I can't ask 'em about it. But I know somebody ran up those piano keys."

Dinah added, "I got proof." She explained that she had just finished dusting and wiping off the keys and had returned to the kitchen. "When I first heard the playin', I was kind of scared to go look for that ghost. But finally I did. And there were his fingermarks right on the keys!"

The whole group raced into the living room to look at the marks. There they were—small, brownish smudges. Harry raced off to get a magnifying glass, and the children took turns looking at the marks.

All were mystified except Bert and Nan, who winked at each other. "Let's keep it a secret," Nan whispered, and her twin nodded.

The next morning when the children came to breakfast Aunt Sarah looked worried. "Mrs. Burns just phoned me," she explained. "Mr. Burns is still ill and they can't get their beans picked. If the beans aren't taken off the vines today, they'll be too big to bring a good price!"

Nan spoke up at once. "Why don't we offer to pick them for her? Maybe we can finish in time!"

"That's very thoughtful of you, Nan," Aunt Sarah observed. "How about it, boys?"

"Sure!" Bert agreed. "And I'll bet Tom and Bud would like to help, too."

When Harry phoned them, the two boys declared themselves eager to pick beans. In a short time they arrived at Meadowbrook farm wearing jeans and big straw hats.

"I want to wear a hat like that!" Freddie declared.

"Me too!" Flossie piped up.

"I'm sure we have sun hats enough for all of you," Aunt Sarah assured her, laughing.

A little later, the five boys and two girls set out for the Burns farm. They all wore blue jeans and large hats. Mrs. Burns was surprised and delighted when Nan told her why they had come.

"Why, you dear children!" she cried. "I declare that's the nicest thing I ever heard of! Wait until I tell my husband. Then I'll get the truck and drive you down to the field."

In a few minutes she backed a pickup truck from the garage, and the children climbed in. When they reached the field, she said, "Each of you grab a bushel basket," and pointed to several piles in a corner of the truck. "When you've filled these, come back for more!"

The farmer's wife showed the children just how to snap off the bean pods without pulling up the plants. "Don't pick any beans smaller than this," she said, holding up a pod for a sample.

"I'll take this row and you take that one," Bert suggested to Harry. "Then we can talk as we move along."

Tom and Bud took the next two rows, then came Nan with the small twins.

"Let's have a race," called Tom. "See who picks a basketful the fastest!"

"You bet," said Bert. "But to make it fair, I think Flossie and Freddie should fill one basket together."

"Okay. Let's go!"

They all set to work, and for a long time no one spoke. The beans were plentiful, and the baskets were filled quickly.

Presently Flossie called out, "We've finished!"

Mrs. Burns, who had been picking too, straightened up and looked over at Freddie and Flossie.

"That's fine!" she called. "Can you carry the basket to the truck or are you tired?"

"We're not tired! Flossie and I are going to pick a million baskets of beans!" Freddie boasted.

They each took a handle of their basket and started toward the truck. But the load was awkward and Freddie stumbled. Down they both went, overturning the container as they fell! Beans flew in all directions!

As Flossie scrambled to her feet, she wailed, "Now we have to pick the same beans twice!"

Nan came over to help and in a few minutes all the beans had been recovered.

"My basket's full!" Bert shouted.

"I'm next!" Tom Holden called.

The boys carried their baskets to the truck, got empty ones and resumed picking. All the baskets were quickly filled, so Mrs. Burns drove them to the barn and returned with additional empty ones.

"You're the best workers I ever had," she said. "I'm inviting you all to lunch."

"We accept," Harry replied with a grin.

Now and then the children stopped to rest. On one of these occasions Nan glanced up at the sky. The sun was directly overhead.

"It must be noon!" she exclaimed. Nan was standing near Flossie, and whispered to her, "I have an idea! Why don't we slip away now? We'll go to the house and get lunch ready."

"That's a scrumptious idea!" Flossie cried. "No one's looking. Let's go!"

When the girls entered the cheerful kitchen, they found Mr. Burns lying on a daybed where he could look out the window.

"I saw you coming," he remarked. "You must be hungry."

Nan explained that she and Flossie had thought they might surprise Mrs. Burns by preparing lunch.

"That would be fine!" Mr. Burns observed. "I've been lying here wishing I could do it, but I'm a little wobbly on my legs!"

"Maybe you can tell us what to get," Nan suggested, going over to the sink to wash her hands.

"Indeed I can," the farmer replied. "It's not very fancy because we didn't know you were coming. But it's good farm food!"

At his direction Nan took a large home-cured ham from the refrigerator. She set it on the big round table covered with a red-and-white checkered cloth. Then Nan carefully sliced a platterful of the spicy pink meat. Flossie brought out two big pitchers of foamy milk.

"Over there in the cupboard," Mr. Burns said, "you'll find some of Mother's homemade bread. I think she makes the best in the county!" In addition to the bread the girls found jars of preserves and jelly.

Mr. Burns now pointed to a big iron bell mounted on top of a pole outside the kitchen door. "That's the farm dinner bell," he explained. "Just pull the rope and your bean pickers will come running!"

Ding Dong! Ding Dong! the old bell rang out. The girls heard the truck start in the distance. In a few minutes, it pulled into the yard and the boys tumbled out.

"Well now, isn't this just wonderful!" Mrs. Burns exclaimed when she saw the neatly set table. "Aren't these good children, Peter?" she asked, tears shining in her eyes.

Mr. Burns nodded in agreement. "They are!"

After everyone's hands had been washed, the group sat down at the table.

"Oh boy, this tastes good!" Freddie cried as he bit into the crusty bread.

When the last piece of bread and the last slice of ham had been eaten, Mrs. Burns got up from the table. "I have a surprise for you," she announced. "I did have some dessert already made."

She walked into the pantry and a minute later returned carrying a tray of cherry tarts.

"Goody, goody!" Flossie chirped. "I love baby cherry pies!"

"They're made from our own cherries," Mr. Burns explained. "They came from that old tree right outside the door!"

Mrs. Burns smiled. "If you'd like to, Freddie, you may pick some to take to your aunt."

Freddie's eyes shone at the prospect. "Thank you, Mrs. Burns," he said eagerly. "That will be neat!"

The cherry tarts were soon eaten, then Bert stood up. "Come on, fellows," he suggested. "There are still beans to be picked!"

Nan and Flossie said they would wash the luncheon dishes and then walk down to the field.

Freddie decided he would stay with the girls. Presently he strolled over to the cherry tree.

"I guess I'll get my cherries now," he thought.

The next minute he had scrambled up to the first limb. Higher and higher he climbed. Soon he was near the top where the cherries had not been picked.

Freddie settled himself on a branch and reached out to pick a red cluster of fruit. "Oh, oh," he thought in dismay. "I didn't bring anything to put the cherries in!"

He thought very hard. It seemed a long way to climb down just to get a basket. "I'll put them down my shirt front," he decided. "When I can't hold any more, I'll go find something to put the rest in."

Freddie picked quickly, stuffing the cherries inside his brown shirt. At length, when there was no more room, he began climbing down.

As he neared the bottom, Freddie decided to jump down. But he lost his balance. *Bang!* Freddie landed face down on the ground!

In the kitchen Nan and Flossie heard the *thump.* Flossie dashed out the door to see Freddie lying motionless in a mass of red!

"Nan!" she screamed. "Freddie is killed!"

At the sound of her cry Freddie sat up unsteadily. "I'm not killed, Flossie," he assured her. "I just—lost my breath—for a minute."

"But you're bleeding!" Flossie insisted.

By this time Nan was bending over her little brother. "It's not blood!" She giggled. "It's cherry juice!"

"I've smashed all my cherries!" Freddie wailed.

When Nan led Freddie into the kitchen, Mr.

Burns sat up, startled. "What happened?" he asked.

Nan explained about the fall and the ruined cherries as she took off Freddie's soggy shirt and washed the red juice from his face and arms and chest.

"I'm glad you're not hurt, young fellow," Mr. Burns said thoughtfully. "There's a paper bucket on the porch if you want to get some more cherries." This time Freddie was very careful and soon had a bucket full of shiny red fruit.

Presently the pickers drove up with a truck-load of beans. They laughed upon hearing the story of "bloody" Freddie.

As the boys climbed out of the truck, Mrs. Burns said, "Wait a minute now and I'll get your money."

"But we don't want any money, thank you," Bert replied. "We picked the beans to help you out!"

The other children nodded vigorously. In spite of Mrs. Burns' insistence, they refused any payment.

"You're really wonderful boys and girls," she exclaimed. "I'll drive you home."

"No, thank you," Harry spoke up. "We'll walk. I know a short cut."

A while later the children climbed a distant stone wall and started across a pasture. Bert suddenly cried out, "Look! There's a bull loose! Is it Major?"

CHAPTER XII

A NEW CLUE

MAJOR! Had the Bobbseys' missing bull broken away from the men who had stolen him? Was he trying to find his way home?

By this time the bull was trotting toward them. Harry looked closely, then suddenly he exclaimed, "That's not Major! The bull belongs to Mr. Hopkins, and it's a mean animal! We'd better run!"

Nan grabbed Flossie's hand while Harry caught Freddie by the arm. They dashed across the field with the other boys close behind.

"Over the fence! Quick!" Harry called.

But all at once Bert's ankle turned and he went down. The others did not see him fall. They scrambled over the fence, then looked back when they noticed Bert was not with them.

"Bert!" Nan screamed. "Hurry!"

As Bert picked himself up, he saw the bull

charging straight toward him. The boy knew he never could reach the fence in time.

"What'll I do?" Bert thought desperately. Then a picture on bullfighting flashed into his mind. The thing the fighter did to keep the bull from charging him was to fool him.

Quickly Bert made up his mind. As the animal lunged toward him, Bert jumped nimbly aside, and the bull plunged ahead. Quick as lightning Bert raced to the wall. By the time the bull could turn around, the boy was safe on the other side.

"Oh, Bert, I was so scared!" Nan sank down limply on the grass.

"Me too!" Flossie gasped.

"That was a close call," Harry commented. "You used your head!"

"I'm sorry the bull wasn't Major," Bert replied. "But you ought to hear something about him soon."

"Bert's a real bullfighter!" Freddie exclaimed admiringly.

"He sure is!" Tom agreed.

"Say!" said Bud. "We ought to have a show. Bert could put on a terrific act."

"That would be fun," Harry agreed. "We could train some of our pets to perform."

"And charge admission and give the money to Skipper!" Nan suggested.

Everyone became enthusiastic about the idea. All the rest of the way home the talk was about the proposed show. It was decided that each child would train an animal to perform.

Bert would teach Rocket a trick. Nan said she had an idea for Frisky, and Harry would think of some way to use his homing pigeons. Freddie volunteered to do something with Snoop and Fluffy. Tom and Bud had goats which they would race.

Only Flossie could think of nothing to enter. "Never mind, honey," Nan consoled her. "We'll help you find an animal trick."

"When and where shall we have the performance?" Harry asked.

"This is Thursday," Bert said slowly. "How about next Tuesday? That would give us enough time to get ready."

This day was agreed upon for the show.

"We can have it at our place," Tom offered. "My dad has a big awning he uses for stock shows. I'm sure he'd put it up for our show. We could have some of the acts under it and use our riding ring for Rocket's trick and the goat race."

"That will be super!" Nan replied.

Before separating, Tom, Bud, and Harry said they would call their friends and spread the news of the forthcoming show around the countryside.

As Harry phoned several children, he asked each one if the boy or girl had seen or heard anything of his stolen bull. The police had not tracked down the thieves, and had no report that Major had been sold.

Harry had no luck until he spoke to a boy named Barry Davis. "Who did you say you think those thieves were?" Barry asked.

"Clint and Mitch."

Barry said excitedly, "I think I saw them."

"Really? Where?"

"I went fishing the other day," Barry answered. "Over at the pond above the Burns place, not far from the dam. I dropped my pole in the water and it floated down. I ran after it, planning to grab the pole at the foot of the dam."

"Yes, go on," Harry urged, as Barry paused.

"Standing near the foot of the dam," Barry continued, "were two men. They were arguing so loudly I could hear some of their words, even though the water coming over the dam was making a lot of noise. The men called each other Mitch and Clint, I'm pretty sure."

"What else did they say?" Harry asked excitedly.

"I only heard words, not sentences. They said 'sell' and 'long wait' and 'smart kids.'"

"Nothing about my bull, Major?" Harry asked.

"I didn't hear anything about him. When the men saw me, they ran away in the woods beyond the dam."

"Barry, that's a swell clue," Harry told his friend. "Thanks a million. Be sure to come to our show. Good-by now."

After Harry finished calling several other friends, he got hold of Bert and Nan and told them what he had learned about Mitch and Clint. The twins were excited.

"Let's go over there and look for those two thieves!" Bert urged.

Without hesitation the three children hurried from the house. Harry led the way back toward the Burns farm, then followed the stream that ran near it all the way to the dam.

"Wow! A lot of water comes over that dam!" Bert remarked. "You don't suppose Major was brought here for a drink and something happened to him?"

"Major was pretty smart, but he could have broken a leg on these stones and drowned," Harry admitted.

"Oh, I hope not," said Nan worriedly. "Let's just think he's all right and look for hoofprints."

"Good idea," Bert agreed. "If we don't find

hoofprints, maybe we can follow the footprints of Mitch and Clint."

The children began a search. They found many animal foot marks, but none of them had been made by a bull. Harry suggested that he and the twins take off their shoes and socks and wade across the stream. They did this, but had no better luck. The three of them were about to give up when Nan spotted men's footprints.

"Two sets of them!" she cried out.

Eagerly she and the boys traced the marks for some distance. They ended at a road running through the woods.

"Those men had a truck here," said Bert. "See the wide tire tracks."

Harry groaned. "Major was probably in it. Maybe Mitch and Clint went to the brook to get water for him."

Without thinking, the children began following the tire tracks. They went on and on. Finally Harry said he and the twins were getting farther and farther from their farmhouse.

"And it's nearly suppertime," Nan spoke up. "Our families will wonder where we are."

"Why don't we go home and phone the police about what we found out?" Bert suggested.

The others nodded. Harry took a short cut through the woods and fields and half an hour later the three children reached Meadowbrook

Farm. At once Harry reported his clue to the police.

The whole Bobbsey family waited hopefully for news that Clint and Mitch had been picked up, but none came. "Those men—and Major—are well hidden," the twins' father said. "But I'm sure they'll be caught sometime."

The next days were busy ones for the children. Besides the farm chores which they did each morning, Bert spent most of his time in the pasture with Rocket. Freddie secluded himself in the basement with Snoop and Fluffy. Nan had taken her mother and Aunt Sarah into her confidence and the three made several trips into town.

Finally, on Monday, Flossie came to her sister with a long face. "I still haven't any animals for the show," she complained. "What am I going to do?"

"There must be some kind of animal here that you can use," Nan replied. "Let's walk around and see what we can find."

They went out to the barnyard. Frisky gave a little jump as they approached and ran as far as her rope would permit. Billy and Betty neighed from their stalls. In the chicken yard the hens clucked busily.

"I can't train any of them!" Flossie cried in despair.

"We'll keep looking. I'm sure we'll find something."

The girls turned toward the orchard. From under a pile of brush at the side a little mouse ran across their path.

"Oh, isn't she darling?" Flossie cried. "Do you s'pose there are any more under that grass?"

The girls bent down and gently lifted the dried brush. In a small hollow was a nest with five tiny mice in it!

"Oh, Nan!" Flossie exclaimed. "Do you think I can capture them?"

"That must have been the mother we saw," Nan replied. "She'll be back. Then maybe we can take all the mice. You stay here and guard them, Flossie. I'll find Harry and see if he has a cage we can put them in."

A few minutes later Nan was back, a broad smile on her face. She carried a wire cage. "Harry once had pet mice," she said. "This was their cage and he says you may use it. Did the mother come back?"

"No."

Nan was sure she soon would. The girls would wait. Carefully Nan and Flossie lifted the baby mice and placed them in the cage through the door. In less than a minute the mother mouse arrived and scurried in with her children. Nan closed the door.

"I'll put the mice on a shelf in the barn," Flossie decided. "Then nothing will hurt them."

The next morning she ran into the kitchen. "May I have some lettuce, Martha?" she pleaded.

"What do you want lettuce for this early in the morning?" Martha asked in surprise.

"For my mice. Harry says mice get their water from greens!"

"Feeding good lettuce to mice!" Dinah exclaimed, and threw up her hands. "Mercy! Don't bring those mice into the house, Flossie!"

The little girl explained that the mice were living in a cage in the barn. "There's a little wheel in the cage and the mice have learned to ride around on it. I'm going to show them this afternoon," she ended proudly.

The day was bright and sunny and the children got to work early. Mr. Holden had set up the awning and just in front of it were to be the seats for the audience.

Folding chairs, garden furniture, and orange crates were collected and put in rows. Patty Manners had agreed to take in the money so she brought along a small wooden box to put it in.

When Mark Teron had heard the plans for the circus, he wanted to help. The bully had promised earnestly not to play any more mean tricks, so the children had decided to let him be the master of ceremonies.

Mark arrived at the Holden farm wearing long black trousers, a striped vest, and an old top hat. He had even painted a curling black mustache on his upper lip, and carried an old-fashioned buggy whip.

"My mother said I should dress for the part," he explained with a grin.

"You look wonderful, Mark!" Flossie commented admiringly.

The time set for the show came, and the audience began to take seats. It was a good-sized crowd. Dinah and Martha settled themselves on two orange crates.

Mark stepped out in front with Harry standing just behind him. "La*deez* and gentlemen!" he called. "There will be a slight delay while we are waiting for the opening act."

The people in the audience looked at one another in amusement. What was holding up the show?

CHAPTER XIII

THE RACE

AS THE audience watched, Harry looked into the sky. All eyes went upward. A pigeon fluttered downward and landed on Harry's shoulder.

The boy stepped forward. As he carefully unfastened a capsule from the bird's leg, he said. "This is one of my homing pigeons. He has brought a message from Mrs. Manily at the Fresh Air Camp."

Harry pulled out the tiny piece of paper and read it. "Mrs. Manily thanks you all for coming to help Skipper and invites you to visit the camp."

Mark spoke up again. "This pigeon was trained by Harry Bobbsey," he explained. "He took it to the camp this morning and Mrs. Manily released it just five minutes ago!"

Everyone clapped loudly.

"The next act," Mark called, "will be Miss

Nan Bobbsey and the Sacred Calf of India!"

From the Holdens' barn came Nan Bobbsey leading Frisky. The calf's back was covered with a piece of red cloth bordered in gold braid. It reached nearly to the ground. Over each ear was tied a long-handled feather duster!

Nan wore a length of thin yellow cloth over her blouse and shorts. It was wrapped around her to resemble an Indian *sari*. At a signal from Nan, Frisky stopped in front of the audience. She nodded her head up and down and pawed the ground.

"That's wonderful!" Aunt Sarah exclaimed. "I didn't know we had such a smart calf!"

There was great applause as Nan led Frisky back to the barn.

"Our next event," Mark said importantly, "is an exhibition of two wildcats straight from the jungle!"

Mark snapped his whip and out came Freddie with a cat on each arm.

"That's our Snoop!" Dinah chuckled. "And Fluffy!"

Solemnly Freddie held his arms out straight in front of him. Snoop and Fluffy carefully walked along them into his hands. Next Freddie crouched down, making a circle of his arms. First Snoop, then Fluffy jumped through!

"Why, Freddie, that's marvelous!" exclaimed his mother.

"You've trained them very well!" added his father.

When the applause died down, Mark snapped the whip again. "And now," he called, "we have the famous performing mice exhibited by Miss Flossie Bobbsey!"

The children in the audience giggled as Flossie walked out from the barn proudly holding the wire cage in front of her. She set it down on a box. The little mice were making the wheel spin at a fast rate.

"These mice are not only acrobats," Mark went on, "but they can also sing!"

"What!" a boy called out.

From inside the barn came a voice which

sounded very much like Bert's, singing *Three Blind Mice*. Even Flossie could not keep from giggling. The applause which greeted this act was the loudest yet.

Then Mark held up his hand. "Now, if you will turn toward the riding ring," he said, "you will see a great exhibition of Wild West riding by that daring cowboy, Bert Bobbsey!"

As directed, the spectators turned in their seats until they faced the riding ring. There were several boxes piled up in the middle. On top of them was a canvas school bag.

Mark moved over to the ring. "You will now see the robbing of the stagecoach!" He indicated the boxes. "This is the coach and on top is the mail!"

At this moment Bert rode into the ring mounted on Rocket. He was dressed in the cowboy suit which he had received the previous Christmas. Bert urged the pony into a trot and circled the ring once. In a few more laps Rocket was going at a steady run. Faster and faster he went. Then Bert got a firm hold on the reins, stood up in the stirrups and pulled alongside the box stagecoach. With a flourish he leaned over, grabbed the school bag, and rode off around the ring.

"Yippee!" Freddie yelled.

"Ride 'em, cowboy!" came from another boy.

Bert waved his hat as he rode from the ring, amid great applause.

"And now," Mark announced, "our last attraction is a chariot race!"

The audience burst into laughter as they saw the chariots. High cardboard fronts and sides had been fastened to two little wagons, each pulled by a goat. Standing in the wagons like charioteers were Tom and Bud. They wore white shirts belonging to their fathers, which hung outside their shorts. Around the boys' heads were bands of ribbon, Tom's yellow and Bud's green.

"One, two, three!" Mark yelled.

At the crack of the whip, the goats were off. The race was twice around the ring. At the end of the first lap Tom was ahead. Then Bud's goat became excited and ran in front of Tom's.

"Foul!" someone yelled.

Bud succeeded in yanking his goat back into line and the two animals raced around the ring.

"Go it, green!" called Bud's father excitedly.

"Come on, yellow!" Mr. Holden urged.

Everyone was on his feet as the chariots rounded the corner into the home stretch.

"Hurry!" Nan screamed as she saw Tom's wagon fall behind.

"Yea, Bud!" Bert yelled, throwing his cowboy hat into the air.

At that moment Bud's goat put on a burst of speed. He passed the finish line just a foot ahead of Tom's entry!

"Mr. Bud Stout is the winner!" Mark announced. "And that is the end!"

The spectators stood up and applauded wildly as the performers lined up to take a bow.

"That's the best show I've seen in years!" Mr. Bobbsey commented with a chuckle.

When the audience had left, the children quickly cleaned up the grounds. Then Mrs. Bobbsey asked, "Would you like to take the money you've made to Skipper now?"

"Oh yes, Mommy," Flossie exclaimed. "And we can see Skipper again!"

It was decided that the Bobbsey men would drive Martha and Dinah home while Mrs. Bobbsey and Aunt Sarah took the children to the Fresh Air Camp.

As the group drove up to the log cabin, there was a lively ball game going on in front of it. When Skipper saw the station wagon, he left the game and ran over.

"How are you, Skipper?" Mrs. Bobbsey inquired.

"Do you like camp?" Freddie asked, jumping out of the car.

"It's great," Skipper said, his eyes shining with happiness.

At this moment Mrs. Manily hurried out of the cabin to greet her guests. When Nan handed her the money for Skipper, she exclaimed, "This is wonderful! I'll keep this for him until he goes home. Thank you all so much!"

"The pigeon arrived at just the right time!" Harry told her.

"I'm glad," Mrs. Manily replied. "Would you all like to look around our camp?"

Before they had a chance to do this, Freddie said, "Mother, Skipper has never ridden in a station wagon. Can't we take him for a ride?"

Mrs. Bobbsey looked at Aunt Sarah and Mrs. Manily. When they both nodded, she replied, "Of course. But we can't be gone long. We'll look around the camp when we get back."

Freddie and Skipper ran and jumped into the front seat of the car. Skipper sat next to Aunt Sarah. Before they started she let him put his hands on the wheel and pretend to drive.

"You're a good driver," Flossie said seriously.

The little boy beamed. "I think I'll be a truck driver when I grow up," he decided.

Aunt Sarah now took the wheel and drove out the camp road. In a little while they came to a hill. At the top was a refreshment stand.

"How about some ice cream?" she asked.

"Oh, yes!" Freddie exclaimed. "I'm hungry and thirsty! Let's have sodas!"

The car was parked on the slope and everyone went inside. The three smaller children scrambled up onto stools at the counter while the older twins and Harry sat at a table with Mrs. Bobbsey and Aunt Sarah.

Everyone ordered his favorite flavor of ice cream. Skipper had a hard time choosing, but finally decided to have strawberry. "It tastes extra good," he explained.

Freddie and Skipper finished first and ran outside. They climbed into the front seat again.

"I guess I'll drive!" Skipper announced, slipping behind the wheel and jiggling it.

His fingers moved the lever into "neutral" position. Then accidentally he kicked the brake release. The station wagon began to roll slowly down the hill!

At that moment Bert and Harry came from the restaurant. The boys were horrified when they saw Skipper and Freddie inside the moving car. They started racing after it.

"Put on the brake!" Harry yelled.

CHAPTER XIV

THE FLOOD

SKIPPER did not know how to put on the brake of the station wagon. He was so excited that he kept turning the steering wheel from side to side. This made the car swerve dangerously.

"Steer into the field!" Bert screamed.

At this point the road leveled off and there were no ditches. Open fields stretched on both sides.

Freddie heard him. He grabbed the wheel and pulled it hard to the right. The car turned into the field, hit a haystack, and stopped!

By this time Nan and her mother and aunt had heard the commotion and joined the boys. They all ran down the road and into the field.

"Are you all right?" Mrs. Bobbsey cried anxiously as the car door opened and Freddie and Skipper jumped out.

"Y-yes," Freddie answered.

Both little boys had bumps on their heads but were otherwise unhurt.

"We're sorry," Freddie said.

Skipper was too frightened to say anything.

"I'm sure it was an accident," Mrs. Bobbsey told the little boy, patting him on the shoulder, "but you must *never* touch anything on a car."

Skipper finally managed to speak. "I'll never, never touch anything again until I'm big enough to drive!" he promised.

"We know you won't, dear," Aunt Sarah said kindly. "Now we'd better take you back to camp or Mrs. Manily will be worried about you."

By the time the party reached the camp the sky was full of dark clouds and the wind had begun to blow hard.

"We're going to have a storm," Aunt Sarah said. "I think we'd better hurry home. We'll see the camp some other time."

They let Skipper out and drove directly to the farm. Just as they reached the house, the clouds burst and the rain came down in torrents. It rained hard all night and was still coming down the next morning when the children got up.

"What shall we do today?" Flossie asked at the breakfast table. "We can't do any 'tective work."

"Let's play in the barn," Harry suggested. "That's always fun on a rainy day!"

"Oh, yes!" Flossie agreed. "We can play in the hay."

When they got to the barn the Bobbsey children climbed to the mow.

"Let's make a 'shoot the chutes,' " Harry suggested.

"How do you do that?" Nan wanted to know.

"I'll show you."

Harry climbed down and looked around the barn until he found a wide plank. This he propped up with one end in the haymow and the other in the filled hay wagon which stood nearby. Then he stood back and looked at his work.

"That's too steep," he decided. "Bert, help me. We'll move the wagon forward a bit."

Together the boys pushed the old wagon up until the slant of the plank was more gradual.

"I'll slide down first," Harry said. He climbed up to the haymow. Then with his knees up under his chin, he crouched on the top of the board.

Pushing against the floor of the haymow, he started himself off. With a *swoosh* he slid down the board into the hay in the wagon!

"Jeepers!" Bert exclaimed. "That does look like fun!"

One after the other all the children tried the

slide. The barn rang with their shouts and squeals.

"One more ride," Harry said finally.

Each child took a turn, with Flossie coming last. The little girl whizzed down so fast that she made a somersault and landed with a *whack* against the side of the hay wagon.

"Oh, Flossie!" Nan cried out, jumping into the wagon. "Are you all right?"

Flossie began to cry. "I hurt."

"Where?"

"Everywhere. I'm all bent up."

Nan was fearful for a moment. She laid Flossie out flat on the hay and asked her to raise each arm and leg in turn. Flossie did so. Finally she smiled. "I guess I'm all unbent now."

The children played hide-and-seek, then cowboy and Indian until lunch time. It was still raining hard. A little later Uncle Daniel was called to the telephone. Then he prepared to leave the house.

"This rain is likely to cause a lot of flooding," he explained. "I'm going to a neighborhood meeting to see what we can do about it."

After he had gone the children played in the house. When supper time came and went and Uncle Daniel had not returned, everyone grew worried.

"I wonder what's keeping him," Aunt Sarah said as she peered out the window. "Oh, here he comes now!" she exclaimed.

The children rushed to the door to meet him. He looked grave.

"I'm afraid the dam is going to break!" Uncle Daniel said grimly.

Aunt Sarah overheard him and gasped. "Why, the Burns house would be swept away!" she exclaimed.

Uncle Daniel nodded seriously.

"How dreadful!" Nan said. "The Burnses have moved out, of course."

Uncle Daniel shook his head. "Mr. Burns was ready to move out if necessary, but Mrs. Burns doesn't want to leave. She told me she has lived there a good many years. The dam hasn't broken yet, and she doesn't think it's going to this time!"

"Oh, I hope she's right," Aunt Sarah said. "But can't something be done to keep the dam from breaking?"

"I'm afraid not." Uncle Daniel added wearily, "We may as well go to bed. There's nothing more we can do tonight. The State Troopers are watching the dam and they'll call if they need me in any rescue work."

Everyone slept fitfully that night. No word came. By morning the rain had stopped but the sky was still gray as lead. After breakfast Uncle

Daniel got ready to go up to the dam again.

"I'll go with you," Richard Bobbsey said.

The older boys and Nan begged to go along. After a short discussion, their parents agreed.

"Let's go then," Uncle Daniel urged. He and the others put on rain gear and left in the station wagon.

After they had gone Freddie whispered to Flossie, "Come down to the basement. I have an idea."

"What is it?" Flossie asked as she followed her twin down the steps and into Harry's workshop.

"We'll build a Noah's ark for your mice," Freddie explained. "Then they can't get drowned if we have a flood."

"Oh, that's wonderful," Flossie said.

For the next hour the small twins were very busy with hammers and nails. When their little ark was finished the twins ran out to the barn for the mice. When they returned through the basement door, they noticed Snoop sleeping peacefully in one corner of the room. But now the cat leaped to his feet. The next moment he had knocked the cage from Freddie's hand. The door opened, and the mice ran out!

Such a commotion! The mice scurried from the basement room and up the stairs, Snoop after them. When they reached the kitchen where Dinah was making cookies she gave one look, screamed, and threw up her hands.

"Flossie! I told you not to bring those mice into the house!" she cried. "Hold Snoop!"

Freddie managed to pick up his struggling pet. Dinah grabbed a broom and swept the little mice out the back door. Then she collapsed into a chair, fanning herself with her apron.

"You've sent the animals out into the flood!" Flossie cried. "We were going to save them with our ark!"

Dinah chuckled. "I saved them from Snoop and I guess that's better!"

All this while the older children had been having an exciting adventure of their own. When they reached the vicinity of the dam, they found the banks of the pond lined with curious onlookers. Peter Burns was among them. He told the Bobbseys that his wife had finally consented to go to a neighbor's house which was on higher ground.

"I got my stock out too," he continued. "But I had to leave the chickens. Their house was already flooded and I couldn't get to them," he said sadly.

"That's a shame," Bert declared.

Just then several State Troopers came along. "Everybody get out of here at once!" one of them called. "The dam is bulging and will go at any minute! Get back up the road out of danger!"

CHAPTER XV

LITTLE DETECTIVES

THE Bobbseys withdrew with the others to a spot some distance up above the dam and waited. In a few minutes there came a heavy crash.

"What was that?" Nan asked fearfully.

"It might have been the dam cracking," said Uncle Daniel tensely.

Harry quickly climbed a tree nearby and peered down the pond. "It doesn't seem to be the dam," he reported. "There's been no rush of water."

The next minute they heard a shout from the State Troopers who had remained nearer the lower end of the pond.

"A giant tree has fallen across the dam," one shouted. "It may have saved the day!"

"Okay for us to come back?" Uncle Daniel shouted.

"Yes."

The Bobbseys ran back. They gazed at the old elm tree which now lay against the great wall of stone.

"The tree roots must have been weakened by the flood," Uncle Daniel explained. "And the tree fell in just the right place to brace the dam."

Although a disaster had been averted, there was still a great deal of land under water. That afternoon Tom and Bud stopped in at the Bobbsey farm. They were wearing high rubber boots.

"We're going down to look at the flood," Tom explained. "You fellows want to come along?"

Bert and Harry accepted at once and ran to get their boots too. The four started out toward town. At a turn in the road they came to a stop. The road was covered deep with water!

"I wish we had a boat," Tom remarked. He looked across the field to the pond. "Hey! There's one!" It was tied to a tree at the water's edge.

"It belongs to Mr. Harold," Bud explained. "Let's ask if we may use it."

The four boys sloshed across the field to the house and received permission.

"You fellows get in, and I'll push off," said Harry.

They rowed along for a while, then suddenly realized they were in a field. The water was still deep enough and the boat went along easily.

"This is something!" Bert exclaimed. "Imagine rowing over a field!"

The landscape looked so different in the flood that in a few minutes the boys were not sure where they were.

Suddenly Tom called out, "Look! Isn't that Mr. Burns's chicken house?" He pointed to a wooden structure bobbing along on the current.

"It sure is!" Harry agreed. "It must have floated off its foundation!"

"And the chickens are still in it!" Bud said in amazement.

"Maybe we can save it," Harry said, rowing faster. "There must be fifty chickens in there!"

The frightened chickens were squawking loudly as they tried to keep their footing in the tossing house.

"If we only had a rope," Tom lamented, "we could pull it in."

Bert had an idea. He opened the bait box in one end of the boat. Within lay a coiled line.

"Let's try this," Bert said as he made a loop in one end. "Pull up as close as you can to the chicken house, Harry."

His cousin rowed as quietly as he could, but the little waves caused by the rowboat kept pushing the henhouse away.

"All right. I think I can get it now," Bert observed.

He threw the line toward the house. But it fell short. He threw it again and again. The third time the loop caught on a corner of the floating coop.

"Good boy!" Tom called. "Now row slowly, Harry, so the house won't tip over."

The chickens cackled and squawked as their house was towed through the water. Finally, a short distance from the Burns house, the rowboat struck bottom.

The boys scrambled out and managed to pull the chicken house onto dry land. Mr. Burns, who had returned home and was watching through the kitchen window, ran down to meet them.

"How can I ever thank you boys?" he said gratefully. "I had given those chickens up for lost!"

As the boys rowed off, Bert said, "I wonder how the Fresh Air Camp stood up under all the rain?"

Aunt Sarah Bobbsey wondered the same thing. After breakfast the next morning, she telephoned Mrs. Manily. Then she reported to the others, "The camp was flooded! I told Mrs. Manily we'd be right over to see how we could help her."

The two Bobbsey men had business in town and could not go at once. So Aunt Sarah, the twins' mother, and the children went. When they reached the camp a sorry sight met their eyes. The ground was covered with mud, most of the tents were down and the railing of the cabin porch was hung with mattresses put there to dry. Altogether the place had a desolate air.

Mrs. Manily came out to greet them. "Could Skipper stay with us till the mud's gone?" Freddie asked immediately.

The director smiled. "Well, one night, anyway," she said.

The Bobbseys learned that many of the children's clothes had floated away and part of the food supply.

"I'm sure we can collect clothes for you," Nan spoke up.

"And we'll bring over vegetables," Aunt Sarah offered.

Bert said, "Harry, how about catching some fish for the campers?"

"You bet."

The next few hours were busy ones for everybody. While the campers helped shovel away the mud and tidy the place, Nan and her mother went from farm to farm and store to store getting new outfits for the boys and girls. Bert had donated his prize certificate for Nan to use. They collected a good quantity, as everyone was eager to assist the Fresh Air children.

Later Aunt Sarah drove over with meat, vegetables, fruit, and clothes for them. Bert and Harry added several fish.

"You are really lifesavers," Mrs. Manily declared happily.

In the meantime Flossie and Freddie had been entertaining Skipper with a ride in the pony cart. Finally they put Rocket into the barn.

"Let's go up in the haymow," Skipper suggested. "That's where I was when Bert found me."

"Okay," Freddie agreed, and the three children climbed up the ladder.

They ran and jumped in the deep hay for awhile, then Skipper suddenly stood still, a strange expression on his face.

"What's the matter?" Flossie asked.

Skipper put a finger to his lips and crept over to the large opening at the end of the mow. The twins followed. When they peered from the open door they saw two men standing on the ground beneath them talking in low tones.

His lips close to the twins' ears, Skipper whispered, "I'm sure those are the men I heard talking when I was hiding here before!"

Freddie's blue eyes opened wide. "You mean Mitch and Clint?"

Skipper nodded.

"Let's get them!" Freddie cried. Quickly the children climbed down the ladder and ran from the barn.

But the men evidently heard them, because when Freddie and Skipper reached the part of the barnyard under the haymow door, the men were gone. The children searched everywhere, but could not find Mitch and Clint.

"We'd better tell Dinah and Martha," Flossie said.

The children ran to the house and told them.

"You'll call a policeman?" Freddie asked.

Martha phoned State Police Headquarters, and soon two troopers came to investigate. The children felt very important upon being questioned. The officers made an examination of the grounds and said Mitch and Clint had walked from the barn to a truck on the road and gone off.

"I wish I'd caught them," said Freddie. "I'll bet they were going to steal a cow."

The troopers smiled and one advised, "You'd better leave catching them to people older than you."

After the officers had gone, Skipper and the small twins felt let down. They sat on the porch just thinking and looking into space.

Then suddenly Freddie said, "I know something little people can do to solve a mystery!"

"What?" Flossie and Skipper asked.

"After everybody's asleep tonight, except us, why don't we tiptoe downstairs and hide and wait for the person who plays the piano?"

"You mean the ghost?" Flossie asked.

"It can't be a ghost," Freddie told her. "Don't you remember Dinah said he made marks on the keys?"

"Yes," Flossie agreed. "All right. Let's do it. But we ought to keep it a secret."

"Sure. Now *don't* go to sleep, Flossie."

"I won't. But if I do, wake me up. And I hope the piano player comes."

Freddie was so afraid he would fall asleep that he decided to put something into his bed to keep him awake. "One of those burrs like Mark put under the pony's saddle would do it," he told himself and ran off to find the prickly pod.

That night it was almost impossible for the twins to remain awake. Skipper fell asleep at once on an extra cot which had been brought into the boys' room.

Flossie dozed. But suddenly she became aware of someone shaking her. "Get up!" Freddie was whispering in her ear. He was standing alongside her.

Rubbing her eyes, Flossie stepped out of bed. Freddie helped his twin put on her bathrobe and slippers. Then the two went into the hall. Bright moonlight streamed through the windows and it was easy for them to find their way down the stairs to the first floor.

There was not a sound in the house. But just as the twins reached the lower hallway, they heard a note played on the piano!

CHAPTER XVI

A FUNNY GHOST

FLOSSIE and Freddie, holding hands excitedly and feeling a little scared, tiptoed across the hall to the door of the living room. By this time the pianist was playing an off-key scale. The moonlight fell directly on him.

"Snoop!" cried the small twins together.

At their shout the cat jumped down and scooted off toward the kitchen. Flossie and Freddie burst into laughter. Tears rolled down Flossie's cheeks and Freddie rocked back and forth on the floor.

The commotion had awakened everyone upstairs except Skipper. One by one they came hurrying down. Uncle Daniel snapped on the light. All were amazed to see the small twins there, giggling so hard they could not talk at first.

Finally Flossie said, "We caught the piano ghost!"

"What!" the others asked.

"I'll get him," Freddie offered. He ran to the kitchen, scooped up Snoop from his box and raced back. "Here he is!"

Nan and Bert looked at each other and winked. Then Nan nodded and said, "Snoop should have been in the show as a piano-playing cat!"

Everyone laughed now, but finally the small twins quieted down. The piano was closed and everyone went back to bed. The next morning at breakfast the story was told to Skipper, Dinah, and Martha.

"Well, I'm sure glad that mystery was solved," said Dinah with a chuckle. "I was gettin' tired of wipin' off that ghost's marks on the piano keys!"

Presently Bert turned toward Nan and Harry. "Say, are we going to let Flossie and Freddie get ahead of us in solving mysteries?"

"No."

"Then let's try to find Major," Bert urged. "We know he hasn't been sold, and the men who stole him are still around, so the bull must be, too."

"Any suggestions where to look?" Nan asked.

"The woods," Harry replied promptly. "There are lots of woods around here, with neat hiding places."

Uncle Daniel spoke up. "A good place to start might be Hopkins Woods. I have to see Mr. Trimble on business this morning. That's near it. Suppose you three come along."

"Maybe Mr. Hopkins has seen Clint and Mitch," Bert suggested, "and we can pick up a clue."

When they were getting ready for the trip, Aunt Sarah said, "Daniel, would you mind taking Skipper back to camp? They'll be expecting him."

"Get your things, little man," Uncle Daniel said with a smile.

Skipper said good-by to Freddie and Flossie and thanked Aunt Sarah for his visit. Then he climbed into the front seat next to Uncle Daniel and the station wagon started off.

Mrs. Manily was out in front of the cabin when the Bobbseys drove up. "Good morning!" she called gaily.

The children looked around at the camp. How different it looked from the day before! The tents had been set up again. The mattresses had disappeared from the cabin railing. And the mud and debris had been cleared from the ground.

"We were busy all yesterday afternoon," the director explained. "We're almost back to normal again."

By this time most of the campers had gathered around the visitors. They were wearing the clothes the Bobbseys had gathered the day before.

"You've made us all very happy," Mrs. Manily declared. "I hope you'll tell all the people who gave the food and clothes how much they're appreciated."

There had been a good deal of whispering among the campers. Now they began to sing:

"We wish you a happy summer,

We wish you a happy summer,

We wish all the lovely Bobbseys

A happy summer!"

"Oh thank you," said Nan. "A happy vacation to you!"

She and Bert and Harry waved pleased good-bys as Uncle Daniel, grinning, started the car and drove away. When they reached the Trimble farm, he turned in. There was no sign of anyone around the dilapidated house. Uncle Daniel parked the station wagon and they all got out.

"Hello!" Harry called. "Are you here, Mr. Trimble?"

There was no answer.

"His car is here," Uncle Daniel observed, pointing to an ancient automobile parked by the side of the house. "Mr. Trimble must be around somewhere."

"Maybe he's in the barn and can't hear us," Nan suggested.

They walked over to the old building and peered inside. It was dusky and there appeared to be no one about. Then they heard a muffled groan.

"Mr. Trimble!" Uncle Daniel called sharply. "Are you in here?"

"Yes," came a faint reply. "Over in the corner, back of the wagon!"

Quickly they ran to the back of the barn where an old wagon loaded with bales of hay stood. There on the floor lay the old farmer.

Bert and Harry and Uncle Daniel helped Mr. Trimble to his feet.

"I'm glad you found me!" the man exclaimed. "I couldn't move!"

"What happened?" Nan asked.

"More bad luck with those two fellers Mitch and Clint. They come here to the barn this morning, asking me for money. Claimed I didn't pay 'em all I owed 'em.

"I said, 'You ran away. Anyhow, I haven't any money.' They didn't believe me and looked in all my pockets. Mitch got mad then and knocked me down."

"How mean!" Nan said. "Did you have any money in the house?"

"A little," Mr. Trimble answered. "Maybe I'd better go see about it."

Harry and his father assisted the old man to his house, while Bert and Nan followed. Mr. Trimble opened the kitchen table drawer. "It's gone! My money's gone!" he said sadly and sank into a chair.

"Did you hear the men say anything that might be a clue to where they may be?" Bert asked.

"Well, I did hear Clint say he was tired of hiding in Hopkins Woods," Mr. Trimble replied, "and he was going to leave the bull. So they've probably gone by this time."

"But not Major!" Harry cried excitedly.

The children were eager to start their search.

They asked Uncle Daniel to join them but he said he must go to town after completing his business with Mr. Trimble. Harry and the twins started off at once.

Presently Bert said, "Is there any abandoned cabin in this woods?"

"A couple," Harry answered. "Why?"

"I don't think Clint and Mitch would have stayed out in the rain if there was a cabin around."

"That's right," said Nan. "Where are they?"

Harry thought a few moments. "One's on top of a hill. The other's near a little stream. I'll see if I can find it. Then we can follow the water."

It seemed to the twins as if they were going in circles as their cousin tried to locate the stream. But finally he called excitedly, "I see it!"

The children followed its course, scrambling over fallen trees and pushing through underbrush. After a while they saw a rough road that paralleled the water. "The loggers must have cleared this to get the lumber out for the sawmill," Harry commented.

"Let's walk on the road," Nan suggested. "Maybe the cabin is on it."

They found the walking easier and made faster time. Suddenly Bert stopped. "That looks like a cabin up ahead," he said.

"You're right," Harry commented. "In case

somebody is there, let's cut around and come up to it from the back."

The cabin was between the road and the stream, so it was not difficult for the children to slip down to the water again and creep up on the little shack from the rear.

The back door was open. While Nan and Harry waited behind a tree Bert approached it stealthily and looked in. He turned toward the others and shook his head. Then he quietly walked back to join them.

"The cabin seems to have two rooms," he whispered. "The back room is empty, but I thought I heard someone talking in the front."

"What shall we do now?" Nan asked. "Clint and Mitch must be here!"

"Let's crawl up under that side window. Maybe we can hear what's going on," her brother proposed.

The three children took their places under the open window. They could make out two men's voices.

"When are we goin' to get out o' here?" one voice whined. "Those two kids almost caught us yesterday!"

"Take it easy, Clint!" a gruff voice replied. "We'll go just as soon as Al gets here with the truck! And don't think I'm going to leave the bull!"

CHAPTER XVII

BERT'S RESCUE

"FOLLOW me!" Bert whispered. He ran a short distance into the woods from the cabin and ducked behind a tree. Nan and Harry were right back of him and also hid.

"What do you make of that?" Harry asked.

"We've found Clint and Mitch!" Bert exclaimed triumphantly.

"But where is Major?" Nan asked in bewilderment. "He can't be in the house!"

"I have a plan!" Bert said. "We must work fast. Mitch said they were leaving as soon as a truck gets here."

"Okay," Harry agreed. "What'll we do?"

Bert suggested that he would scout around the surrounding area to see if he could find where the stolen bull was hidden. Nan and Harry would stay where they were and watch the cabin.

161

"If you see the men leave, get a good description of the truck," he completed his instructions.

"You'll be careful, won't you, Bert?" Nan asked fearfully as her twin started off through the woods. Her brother turned and with a grin raised two fingers in a V for victory sign!

Bert made a wide circle around the cabin. Although he searched carefully among the trees, there was no sign of the bull.

"Those thieves must have Major hidden somewhere near here!" he thought desperately.

Just then he noticed an odd-looking group of bushes. They were very thick, and as he looked more closely Bert noticed that they were not rooted to the ground.

"That's queer!" he said to himself as he crept nearer. "Maybe they're hiding something!"

When he came up to the bushes, he peered among the withered leaves. Back of the bushes was a strongly built pen. The boy's ears caught a movement on the other side, then he heard a loud stomping sound like hoofs pawing the ground.

"Major!" Bert thought.

He made his way to the other side and pushed among the bushes. Inside the pen, tossing his head and moving restlessly about, was a handsome bull!

"I'll have to find a telephone and call the

troopers!" Bert thought excitedly as he turned away.

"Not so fast, young man!"

Bert jumped. He had been thinking so hard that he had not noticed a stocky, sunburned man step from behind a tree.

"Wh-who are you?" Bert asked nervously.

"None of your business," the man replied gruffly. "But it looks like you're stickin' your nose in *my* business so I guess you'd better come along with me."

Bert started to run, but the burly man stuck out his foot and tripped him. Then he pulled the boy to his feet. Before Bert had a chance to yell, he clapped a hand over his mouth, and dragged him toward the cabin.

When they went in, a thin, swarthy man got up from a stool on which he had been seated. "Who've you got there, Mitch?" he whined. "We don't want nobody else around here!"

"You bet we don't!" Mitch agreed. "But this kid was snoopin' around the bull, so I thought we'd better see that he didn't go no place for a while."

With those words he pushed Bert into a chair. "Get me that rope, Clint!" he ordered.

Meanwhile, Nan and Harry had watched Bert go off through the woods. They caught a glimpse of him now and then as he searched among the trees. Then he had disappeared. Time dragged by.

"I wonder where he is now," Nan asked finally. "I wish he'd come back!"

"Bert told us to stay here," Harry said. "But if we don't see him in a minute, I vote we go look for him!"

The minute passed and the two were just about to walk toward the cabin when they heard the sounds of a scuffle.

"Oh, look!" Nan cried. "That man is taking Bert into the shack!"

"I'll get him!" Harry said angrily, starting to run.

"No!" Nan caught her cousin by the arm. "They'll catch you too! We must get Dad and Uncle Daniel!

Harry stopped. "I guess you're right, Nan."

The two children raced down the rough road, crossed the stream, then cut through several fields. They ran as long as they could, then were forced to slow to a walk.

"I didn't realize it was so far," Nan panted.

"We're almost home," Harry encouraged her. "The house is just over the next hill."

The two children began to run again and in a few more minutes collapsed breathless on the front steps of the farmhouse.

Aunt Sarah rushed out to the porch. "What's the matter?" she cried.

"Bert's been captured!" Nan managed to say.

By this time the rest of the family had reached the porch. The twins' father demanded the rest of the story quickly.

"We must save Bert!" Nan finished desperately.

Mrs. Bobbsey grew pale and grasped her husband's arm. "Oh, Dick! Hurry!"

Uncle Daniel had already run into the house. In a short time he was back. "I've called the State Troopers," he said. "They'll meet us at the cabin. Nan, you and Harry show your father and me exactly where it is!"

The four dashed toward the car and sped along the road toward the thieves' hide-out.

"I know that logging road," Uncle Daniel remarked. "I think it joins this highway just up ahead." He swung into the side road and they bounced along on its rough surface.

"There's the cabin!" Harry shouted.

Uncle Daniel slammed on the brakes. "You two stay here," he instructed as he and Nan's father jumped from the car.

The two men ran into the cabin, but soon came out. "No one's here!" Mr. Bobbsey called.

Nan and Harry dashed over to join their fathers. It was true. The cabin was empty! Harry raced around the side. He found the pen, but it, too, was empty!

"They must have driven away in that truck Mitch was talking about," Harry said in despair.

"And taken Bert with them!" Nan cried. "Oh, Dad, we must find those men!" She was almost in tears.

"Don't worry, Nan. We'll get them!" Mr. Bobbsey's voice was grim.

At that moment two State Troopers drove up. They introduced themselves as Becker and Keller. When they learned that Mitch and Clint had escaped, the officers shook their heads.

"Those men are pretty slippery customers," Becker commented. "There's been a lot of cattle stealing around here lately and we're pretty sure these fellows Mitch and Clint have been doing it."

"What's the next move?" Uncle Daniel asked.

"Maybe we can pick up the truck's tire tracks," Nan spoke up.

"Let's see what we can find," Keller said.

Carefully the six searched the rough logging road in front of the cabin. "Here are some tracks which look as if a truck might have turned around," Harry said finally.

After examining the marks in the dirt, the troopers agreed. "Get in our car," Becker suggested. "We'll see if we can follow those men."

For a while the tracks were fairly easy to spot. Several times they disappeared but were soon picked up again.

When Becker had driven about a mile, the logging road ended at a main highway. The trooper stopped the car. "Which way now, I wonder?" he said.

Nan, Harry, and Keller hopped out of the car. They ran out onto the road and bent over to examine tire tracks, trying to pick up the lost trail. But there had been a great many cars and trucks along the road and it was impossible to tell one mark from another.

"Well, suppose we turn right," Uncle Daniel proposed. "Blaisdell is in that direction. Perhaps the thieves will try to dispose of Major at the stock auction there."

Nan and Harry got back into the car and Becker drove down the road. After about twenty minutes he pulled into a gasoline station.

"I know the manager here," the trooper explained. "Perhaps he's seen a truck with a bull in it.

"Hi, Jim!" Becker called as a jolly-looking man came up to the car. He explained their errand, but the attendant could not help them.

"I've been working on my books," Jim said, "and haven't paid much attention to passing trucks."

They thanked the man and turned out onto the highway again. A few miles farther on, Nan suddenly pointed ahead. "Oh! Isn't that Bert walking up the road toward us?"

"It sure is!" Mr. Bobbsey exclaimed in relief. When the car drew alongside the boy, his father jumped out.

"Well, son," he cried happily, "I'm glad you got away from those kidnapers!"

"Oh, Bert! What happened to you?" Nan asked as her brother climbed wearily into the troopers' car. "We saw that man drag you into the cabin, but when we got Dad and Uncle Daniel and came back, everyone was gone!"

Bert explained that Mitch and Clint had tied him to a chair until a truck arrived. Then they had an argument about what to do with him.

"Clint voted to leave me in the cabin," Bert said. "But Mitch was afraid I'd be found too soon. I had told him I was alone, but I don't think he believed me. He suspected that someone would miss me and spread the alarm."

"Did you find Major?" Harry asked anxiously.

"Yes," Bert replied, "in a pen. When the men were ready to leave they blindfolded me. I was told to climb into the cab of the truck. After that I heard them drive Major up into the back."

"How did you get away?" Uncle Daniel asked.

"They let me out a little while ago. Mitch warned me not to take the blindfold off until I had counted to fifty!"

"Too bad we don't have a description of the truck," Keller exclaimed in disappointment.

"I can give you one," Bert said. "I got a look

at it out the cabin window before they put the blindfold on me. I saw the license plate and memorized the number!"

CHAPTER XVIII

BLUE RIBBON PRIZE

"GOOD boy!" Keller exclaimed. He drew a notebook from his pocket. "Let's have it!"

Quickly Bert described the truck and gave the number of the license. Keller spoke into his two-way radio and relayed the information to headquarters.

"They'll broadcast the description," the trooper explained. "We should have that truck before night unless those thieves hide out someplace else."

"We'll drive you back to the cabin to pick up your car, then we'll be on our way," Becker said to the Bobbseys.

When Uncle Daniel drove up to Meadowbrook Farm a little later, and the anxious watchers on the porch saw Bert get out, a cheer went up. Flossie and Freddie dashed down and threw their arms around their brother.

171

"Oh, you're safe!" Flossie cried. "I was afraid the bad men would take you away forever!"

Bert chuckled as he rumpled his little sister's hair. "I was just playing detective like you," he teased.

His mother and aunt both gave him a warm hug. Then Freddie begged to hear what had happened.

Bert was just finishing his account when the thieves' truck drove into the lane. At the wheel was Trooper Keller.

"This your bull, boy?" the policeman asked with a grin when Harry, followed by Bert, ran down to meet him.

"That's Major!" Harry replied joyfully as he peered into the back of the vehicle.

Keller leaned over and opened the cab door. "Jump in," he said, "and show me where Major lives."

The cousins climbed in and directed the trooper to the barn. The ramp was let down from the truck and Harry led the prize bull into his pen.

"Where did you find him?" Harry asked as they rode back toward the house.

"That was quick service, wasn't it?" Keller asked with a grin. "Becker will be along in a minute with the thieves. Then you can hear the whole story."

By the time Harry and Keller reached the front porch of the farmhouse, a police car was parked there. Becker was driving with another trooper beside him. In the back seat were Mitch, Clint, and a stranger handcuffed together.

"Are these the men you saw in the cabin?" Becker asked Bert as the boy went up to the car.

"Yes, sir," Bert replied, pointing to the stocky, red-faced man. "That's Mitch, and he's Clint," he said, nodding toward the thin swarthy one. "I think that third man is Al, the truck driver."

"We have their full names at headquarters," the other trooper declared. "These three have been in prison for stealing cattle. They just can't seem to learn!"

"Thanks for identifying these crooks," Becker said to Bert as he started the car again. "I'll take them on to jail. Your information led to their capture. They were picked up with Major as they drove into Blaisdell."

Keller got back into the truck and followed the police car down the driveway.

Dinah and Martha had cooked a particularly delicious dinner to celebrate Bert's return. The table conversation was lively as Harry and the older twins again described their adventure.

"You children are very good detectives," Mrs. Bobbsey commented, "but I'm glad you've solved the mysteries of Meadowbrook Farm without anyone's getting hurt!"

"I'd like to have another mystery to solve," Nan said dreamily.

Her mother smiled. "I have a mystery for you."

"What is it, Mommy?" Flossie asked.

"I had a letter this morning that concerns all of us," Mrs. Bobbsey teased. "Can you guess who wrote it?"

There were many guesses until Freddie piped up, "Aunt Emily!"

"You get the prize, Freddie!" Aunt Sarah laughed as she passed him a plate of mints.

"What did Aunt Emily say that concerns us all?" Nan wanted to know.

"I'll bet she's inviting us for a visit!" Bert observed. "That would be keen!"

Aunt Emily Minturn was Mrs. Bobbsey's sister. She lived at Ocean Cliff with her husband and daughter Dorothy who was just Nan's and Bert's age. The Bobbseys always enjoyed visiting the Minturns.

"Ooh!" Flossie exclaimed. "We can go bathing in the ocean. I like that 'cept when the big waves knock me down!"

Freddie snorted. "Why, that's fun! How soon do we go?"

"You can't go until you've been to the County

Fair and see Major get another prize," Harry spoke up.

He explained that the fair would open the following Tuesday. "I've received permission to put in a late entry. The chairman has been holding a place for me in case Major was found."

"That's great!" said Bert. "Mother, may we stay?"

"Oh yes, you must," Aunt Sarah insisted. "Besides, I want to give a farewell party for you."

"Goody! Goody!" Flossie exclaimed.

Harry said Major would need a lot of grooming to make him a show animal. That Monday he and Bert spent several hours in the barn curry combing and brushing the bull until his coat glistened. He even permitted his hoofs to be painted.

"The judges make their decisions tomorrow, and the following day, Wednesday, pin the ribbons on the prize-winning animals," Harry explained. "After Dad and I get Major settled in his pen at the fair, we'll give him another slicking up."

Excitement ran high as everyone at Meadowbrook rode over to the fair on Wednesday. They went at once to see their bull.

"Boy, oh boy!" cried Freddie. "Major won a blue ribbon! Is that first place?"

"Yes, it is," Nan answered. "Isn't it wonderful?"

Everyone congratulated Harry, who had taken care of Major since he was a calf. The bull seemed to sense that he had done something worthwhile. He snorted a little, pawed the ground, and let the children pet him.

At last the twins' mother said if they wanted to see anything else at the fair, they must leave. Finally everyone was tired and they went home.

After lunch and a rest, it was time for the farewell party to begin. All the children who had been on the picnic had been invited—even Mark Teron.

"Mark's all right now," Bert had spoken up in the boy's defense. "He did a good job as master of ceremonies at our show!"

"That's right," Aunt Sarah had agreed. "I'm sure Mark has realized that he has a better time when he behaves himself!"

About two-thirty the guests began to arrive. The boys wore shorts instead of their usual dungarees and the girls looked pretty in crisp cotton dresses.

Aunt Sarah had arranged several games to play and soon the air was full of squeals and giggles and shouts as the children threw darts and played horseshoes.

Finally Mrs. Bobbsey pinned a large picture of a bull to the big maple in front of the porch. "This is Major," she announced, "and the object of this game is to pin the blue ribbon on his ear!"

Aunt Sarah passed around blue paper ribbons with a pin stuck in each. Then one by one the children were blindfolded, spun around, and given a chance to pin the ribbon on the bull. Ribbons began to decorate every part of the animal's body except his ear!

Bert was the last to try. He staggered about, finally heading for the steps. "No, Bert!" Flossie screamed. "You're going the wrong way!"

Bert turned and after a little fumbling pinned his ribbon exactly on the bull's ear!

"Good for you, Bert!" Tom Holden cried. "You can find Major every time!" There were cheers for Bert.

After a while the children were invited into the dining room where there were all kinds of sandwiches, delicious ice cream, and two big layer cakes.

When they were finished eating, Nan announced that her family was leaving the next day.

"Oh, that's a shame," said Patty. "When you Bobbseys are around we have such exciting adventures!"

"Even when we're playing hide-and-seek on a picnic," Kim added happily.

Flossie perked up. "Yes, it was fun, 'cept I was scared when I fell down the cliff!"

"Freddie took a big spill, too," Nan added, "but his had a little more color!"

Freddie giggled. "Yes, next time I want some cherries from a tree, I'll eat all I pick!"

"Oh, you'll get a tummy ache," said Flossie.

"Then I'll ask someone to climb up with me to help pick."

"Don't ask me," Bert popped up. "I have enough trouble rescuing chickens in a flood and finding missing prize bulls!"

The children laughed heartily. Then Harry

broke in. "It seems every Bobbsey got into trouble except Nan."

"I'm just lucky," she said shyly. With that Nan turned suddenly to get up from the table. The chair legs caught on the edge of the rug and she toppled sideways, chair and all!

"Wow!" shouted Freddie as he and the others jumped up in surprise.

"Are you all right?" Bert asked, helping up his twin.

Nan blushed, then grinned as she sat down again. "I guess I'm not so lucky after all!"

The children were ready to leave the table when Aunt Sarah came into the room with tiny favors for each one. They eagerly opened their packages and filled the room with sighs and exclamations.

"This is the most wonderful party I've been to!" Patty cried. "I hope you Bobbseys come to Meadowbrook again soon!"

"We will! We will!" the twins chorused.